P9-CRO-980

SPY
PENGUINS
THE SPY WHO LOVED ICE CREAM

THE SPY WHO LOVED iCE CREAM

SAM HAY

Illustrated by **MAREK JAGUCKi**

FEIWEL AND FRIENDS • NEW YORK

A FEIWEL AND FRIENDS BOOK
An Imprint of Macmillan Publishing Group, LLC
120 Broadway, New York, NY 10271

Printed in the United States of America by
LSC Communications, Harrisonburg, Virginia.

Library of Congress Cataloging-in-Publication Data
Names: Hay, Sam, author. | Jagucki, Marek, illustrator.
Title: The spy who loved ice cream / written by Sam Hay ; illustrated by Marek Jagucki.
Description: First edition. | New York, NY : Feiwel and friends, 2019. | Series: Spy penguins ; [2] | Summary: Jackson, code-named Secret Agent 00Zero, and his inventor-friend, Quigley, both penguins, must prove Uncle Bryn is innocent of robbery before the Frosty Bureau of Investigation locks him away forever.
Identifiers: LCCN 2019001561 (print) | LCCN 2019002959 (ebook) | ISBN 9781250188618 (E-book) | ISBN 9781250188588 (hardcover) | ISBN 9781250188618 (eBook)
Subjects: | CYAC: Spies—Fiction. | Penguins—Fiction. | Brainwashing—Fiction. | Robbers and outlaws—Fiction. | Best friends—Fiction. | Friendship—Fiction. | Humorous stories.
Classification: LCC PZ7.H31387385 (ebook) | LCC PZ7.H31387385 Sp 2019 (print) | DDC [Fic]—dc23
LC record available at https://lccn.loc.gov/2019001561

Book design by Carol Ly
Feiwel and Friends logo designed by Filomena Tuosto
First edition, 2019

1 3 5 7 9 10 8 6 4 2
mackids.com

FOR QUINTEN AND ELLIOT
AND ICE CREAM CONNOISSEURS
EVERYWHERE

SPY
PENGUINS
THE SPY WHO LOVED ICE CREAM

Secret Agent 00Zero (also known as Jackson to his mom) took a deep breath and opened the gate into Mrs. Hoppy-Floppy's yard. He glanced around nervously; he knew they could be under attack at any moment . . .

"Wait until you see what I've got in my bag," his best friend, Quigley, said, following him through the gate. "I've been working all night and—"

"Wait," Jackson interrupted. He squinted up at the sky. The strange-looking cloud he'd noticed a few minutes before was getting bigger. And closer. And . . . flatter? Jackson felt a tingle in his beak as his danger detectors went off. "Does that cloud look weird to you?"

"Huh?" Quigley (also known as Secret Agent Q to Jackson) glanced up. "Nah, it looks like a regular nimbostratus, approximately a thousand flippers high, suggesting it may rain soon.

But anyway, you've got to see what I've come up with."

Quigley began rummaging in his backpack, but Jackson was still distracted by the cloud. There was definitely something odd about it. It was kind of . . . wriggling!

"Agent Q!" Jackson said, grabbing his buddy's flipper. "I think we'd better move."

"What?" Quigley blinked up at the sky.

"RUN!" Jackson shouted. "Enemy attack!" He tugged Quigley across the yard. They dived over a low fence, ninja rolled through some prickly bushes, and threw themselves behind Mrs. Hoppy-Floppy's wheelbarrow just as a huge, squawking flock of gulls swooped down from the sky.

"Ha!" Jackson shouted, waggling his flipper at the gulls. "You missed us!"

"Um . . . not quite." Quigley pointed to Jackson's head.

"Urgh!" Jackson shook the lumps of sticky white poop out of his crest and shuddered. "I hate gulls!"

"I don't think they like us much, either," Quigley said. "That's the third time they've gunked us this week, which is exactly why I've been working on these new gadgets. Let me get them out . . ."

Jackson sighed. This was all his mom's fault. It had been her idea to send them deck scrubbing as punishment for sticking their beaks into FBI business. Joining the FBI (the Frosty Bureau of Investigation) was what Jackson wanted more than anything else in the world.

And after solving the case of the stolen fish from Rookeryville's City Aquarium, the head of the FBI had very nearly made his wish come true—until Jackson's mom found out. She definitely DID NOT want them to be secret agents. Too dangerous, she said. And because they'd broken her rules and gotten involved in spy business, she'd flipped! She'd gone Great White on the Shark Scale of Crossness and put Jackson and Quigley on the worst punishment duty she could dream up: scrubbing gull poop off their neighbors' decks for the whole midterm vacation. And Mrs. Hoppy-Floppy's deck was the poopiest of all.

"Coo-eee!" called an old-lady penguin voice, and Mrs. Hoppy-Floppy emerged from her house, waving to them across the yard. "I'm just filling the gull feeders. Keep up the good work, boys."

Jackson and Quigley waved back.

"I wish she wouldn't feed them," Jackson muttered as Mrs. Hoppy-Floppy waddled off. "Then her deck wouldn't be so covered in poop!" As he spoke, the flock of gulls swooped back down to gobble up the food. "Look at them!" Jackson groaned. "They're like pooping machines! We're going to be here all day. No way are we going to make Uncle Bryn's birthday party."

Uncle Bryn wasn't just Jackson's favorite family member; he was also a real, live secret agent with the FBI. And today was his birthday. Uncle Bryn had planned a small party with a few FBI friends down at Brain Freezers, the best milk shake shack in all of Rookeryville. And Jackson and Quigley were invited, too. Not that they were allowed to go, of course. They were still grounded as part of Jackson's mom's punishment plan. But Jackson had a plan of his own. He knew his mom was at work until 6 P.M. and his dad was busy building a new game room in their basement, so Jackson figured they could sneak down to the party without anyone finding out. But first they had to finish scrubbing Mrs. Hoppy-Floppy's deck.

"Don't worry," Quigley said. "I've been trying to tell you. I've been working on some awesome new deck-scrubbing inventions. They'll get the job done quicker. Check these out!"

Jackson peered at the flowery bits of fabric Quigley was waggling in front of him. "They look a lot like your nana's old curtains."

"They ARE my nana's old curtains," Quigley said. "Or they were, until last week. Now they're my latest and greatest invention—Poop Protector Hats! See, you put them on like this and—"

"Why have they got spoons attached?"

Jackson asked, crossing his flippers in the hope he wouldn't have to wear one.

"They're not spoons. They're poop splatterers. See, you press this button here," Quigley said, fiddling with the top of the hat, "and they spin around. Then if a gull drops poop on you, it gets batted away. Genius, right?"

Jackson nodded. "Um . . . sure."

"I've got more," Quigley said, rummaging in his bag again. "Ta-daaa!"

"Skates?" Jackson's sister, Finola, had a pair just like them. Except Finola's definitely did not have brushes attached to the bottoms.

"Robo SCRUB Skates!" Quigley corrected. "Look, I'll show you."

Jackson kept his eyes on the gulls as he followed Quigley across the deck to the dirtiest area, where the birds were pecking at the seeds Mrs. Hoppy-Floppy had put out for them.

"So you tie the Robo Scrub Skates on your feet like this," Quigley said, "then flick the switch on the back, and—*whoa!*" He steadied himself as the skates began to twitch and shudder. "See? They do all the scrubbing for you! Awesome, right?"

Jackson jumped out of the way to avoid being trampled by his friend, who was now jerking backward and forward wildly as the skates scrubbed the deck's boards.

"Oh, and you're going to love this . . . ," Quigley shouted. "Catch!"

Jackson caught the small silver object his buddy had thrown. "A whistle?"

"Blow it!" Quigley said.

Jackson did as he was told. "I don't hear anything."

The gulls had heard something, though. They'd stopped pecking and spun around to stare at Jackson.

"It's a Gull Scarer! Only gulls can hear it. And they hate it!" Quigley pulled out another whistle. As he blew it, the gulls began to squawk and shuffle around, fluttering their wings. Two of them flew away.

"Wow," Jackson breathed. "You really are

a genius." He reached for the second pair of skates. *Who cares if we look lame,* he thought, pulling them on and picking up the other crazy hat. *At least there's no one here to see it.* "Hey, maybe Uncle Bryn's boss will be at the party," Jackson said, his feet now jerking backward and forward as the spoons spun wildly around his hat. "Then we can remind her about her idea to start a junior wing of the FBI."

But Quigley didn't reply. He was staring at the sidewalk outside Mrs. Hoppy-Floppy's house. "I think that penguin just took a photo of us."

"What penguin?" Jackson tried to turn to look, but his Robo Scrub Skates had other ideas. Jackson went one way, his feet went the other. And—*doof!*—his face hit the deck.

"Hey, loser patrol!" shouted a familiar, annoying voice. "LOVE the hats!"

Jackson scrambled back up and locked eyes with—

"Hoff Rockface!" he growled. Their number-one enemy from school.

Hoff turned and called to his friends down the street. "Hey, dudes, come check out these losers."

Jackson felt his cheeks burn. He tried to pull the flowery hat off his head, but the spoons were rotating so fast he couldn't grab it. "Quigley!" he hissed. "How do I get this off?"

But before Quigley could answer—

"Smile for the camera!" Hoff took another picture of them.

"Stop that!" Jackson yelled. "You can't take our photo!"

"Why not?" Hoff looked offended. "I'm just doing my school vacation homework. You've done yours, right?"

Jackson glanced at Quigley. "*Homework*?" he mouthed.

Quigley shrugged.

Hoff sniggered. "Did you guys forget? Miss Chalk-Feather is *not* going to be happy."

Miss Chalk-Feather was their new teacher. She was a super-strict sort of penguin, almost as strict as Jackson's mom.

"We've got to make a *Visitor's Guide to Rookeryville,* showing all the best sights in town," Hoff said, talking slowly, like he was speaking to hatchlings.

Jackson groaned. *Now* he remembered! Miss Chalk-Feather had said they could make any kind of guide they wanted—a drawing, a leaflet, a photo display, or anything else. Jackson and Quigley had buddied up to do theirs together, then immediately forgotten about the assignment.

Hoff pointed his camera at Jackson again. "Well, you and Gadget Boy are definitely appearing in my *Visitor's Guide to Rookeryville.* You're the freakiest sight in town. Smile!"

Jackson felt a bubble of anger in his belly. NO WAY was he appearing in Hoff's homework. "Code Red!" he hissed at Quigley. "Quick! We've got to get that camera off him!"

Jackson lunged toward Hoff. But every time he moved, the skates scrubbed him backward.

Hoff and his friends exploded with laughter.

"Quigley!" Jackson hissed. "Do something!"

"Don't worry," Quigley said, pulling out a remote control. "I'll flick the switch to turbo mode!"

"What? *Argh!*" Rocket blasters shot out of the back of Jackson's skates and thrust him forward.

Hoff had stopped laughing. His eyes widened as Jackson, his hat spinning and his feet flying, came thundering toward him.

"Ahhhh!" Jackson yelled, even though he was breaking the basic rule of secret-agent survival: NEVER scream like you're scared!

But seeing as Jackson WAS scared, because he was heading straight for Mrs. Hoppy-Floppy's wooden fence, which was between him and Hoff, with no way of stopping, he couldn't help it. "Arghh!" he screamed louder. *Got to jump it!* Jackson told himself. *Got to jump the fence!*

But instead of jumping it, he *THWUMPED* it.

BAM!

Jackson opened his eyes and gave his feathers a shake. *Nope. No bones broken.* And considering he'd just blasted halfway through a wooden fence at turbo speed, that was a pretty good outcome.

"Selfie!" Hoff's horrible face suddenly appeared next to his. "Smile for the camera!"

"What? No! Stop!"

But Hoff had already taken the photo. "Nice one, Jackson. You're a loser legend. Come on," he called to his friends. "I can't wait to post this on the school blub."

Jackson gritted his beak. The school had a

new Ice-net blub page where students could share news and events. Jackson groaned. He did NOT want to be today's headline story. He tried to scramble to his feet, then tripped over his skates and landed back in the broken fence. He could hear Hoff and his friends laughing their feathers off as they shuffled away.

"Oh, wow!" Quigley said, peering down at Jackson's head. "That crash-helmet inner lining I installed on the Poop Protector Hat really worked. See? There's not a mark on your head. Well, apart from two bent spoons. But I can fix them."

"Great!" Jackson tugged off the hat and skates and hauled himself up. "Shame you didn't install a Hoff-zapping device in it, too!" He looked at the broken fence, then over at the poopy deck, where even more gulls had arrived. "Guess we're not going to make Uncle Bryn's birthday party."

"Hello? Is everything okay?" They turned to find Mrs. Hoppy-Floppy standing behind them.

"Oh, um—hi." Jackson felt his face go shrimp pink. "I'm—err, so sorry about your fence. You see, we were trying out some new deck-scrubbing equipment—"

"My new inventions!" Quigley interrupted. "To get the job done faster."

"But they went a bit wrong and—"

"It's all right," Mrs. Hoppy-Floppy said. "But I think that's enough deck scrubbing for today. In fact, I think that's enough for the rest of the vacation."

"But what about your fence?" Jackson began. "We can fix it—"

"No!" Mrs. Hoppy-Floppy interrupted. "Absolutely not!" She steadied herself against the remaining fence post. "It's very kind of you to want to help, but my son will fix the fence. Why don't you boys go home now?"

Jackson couldn't believe his ears. "Are you sure?"

Mrs. Hoppy-Floppy nodded.

"And you won't tell his mom?" Quigley added.

"I'll tell her you were very helpful," Mrs. Hoppy-Floppy said. "So helpful that you never need come help again!"

"That was strange," Quigley whispered as they shuffled away. "It was almost like Mrs. Hoppy-Floppy didn't want our help."

"At least we won't miss the party," Jackson said, picking up his ice cycle from the grassy bank where they'd parked them. "Come on! Let's do this!"

The boys ducked their heads as they cycled past Jackson's house, just in case his dad was looking.

"Hey, was that a heli-hopper pad on the roof of your house?" Quigley said.

"Yeah, Dad just finished it." Jackson's dad loved to build new rooms onto their house. Last week, he'd added a smoothie-juicing room next to the kitchen, and before that he'd built a pottery-making den under the stairs. But the heli-hopper pad was Jackson's favorite; all secret agents needed to know how to fly a heli-hopper. "We haven't actually gotten a heli-hopper yet," Jackson explained. "But—"

"I could build you one!" Quigley interrupted. "Sunny could help me."

Jackson wobbled on his ice cycle. "N-n-no, it's okay, but thanks." Quigley's big cousin

Sunny was an even more dangerous inventor than Quigley. "So what are you going to order at Brain Freezers?" Jackson asked, changing the subject. "A triple-choc seaweed shake, maybe?"

They spotted Uncle Bryn as they pulled up outside the café.

"Cool! He bagged the window booth," Quigley said, chaining his ice cycle to a lamp-post. The window booth was their favorite seat at Brain Freezers. Mission Control, as they called it, was where Jackson and Quigley liked to plan their adventures.

"I don't see his boss, though," Jackson said. "Maybe she's coming later. Hey, Uncle Bryn," he called as they walked into the café. "Happy birthday!"

But his uncle didn't look up. Neither did his two colleagues. They just sat there staring straight ahead, spooning weird-looking ice cream into their beaks.

"Happy birthday, Uncle Bryn!" Jackson tapped him on the back. Still no response. Jackson glanced at Quigley, who shrugged. "Guys?" Jackson looked across the table at Uncle Bryn's work friends. But they just kept eating their ice cream—a strange-looking sort that Jackson had never seen before. It had yellow and green stripes, and—Jackson blinked—it glowed! "What flavor is that?" Jackson asked them.

But no one replied. No one moved. They just kept eating and staring.

"Maybe they're playing a party game?" Quigley whispered. "Like ice statues."

But Jackson didn't think so. His beak tingled. His danger detectors were going off again. There was something odd happening here. He just knew it.

"I like your new cap, Mr. Rockflopper," Quigley said to Jackson's uncle Bryn. "Did you get it for your birthday? Oh, wait, I see you've all got one." He nudged Jackson. "Hey, maybe they're giving caps away here today. I'll ask Victor." Quigley looked around the diner. "I don't see Victor, do you?"

Victor was the manager of Brain Freezers. He always liked to greet the customers himself.

"I don't see anyone I recognize," Jackson muttered. He stared at the two people serving behind the counter. They were both wearing the same sort of cap as Uncle Bryn and his colleagues, blue with a letter *F* embroidered on the front. "They must have hired new staff."

Uncle Bryn laid down his spoon and stood up. His two colleagues did the same. They pushed past the boys, heading for the door.

"Wait—Uncle Bryn," Jackson called. "Where are you going?"

But his uncle didn't reply. He kept walking, zombie-style, out the door.

Jackson and Quigley followed the agents out onto the sidewalk.

"Uncle Bryn! What's going on?" Jackson had a funny feeling in his tummy now—a sort of knot. Uncle Bryn NEVER ignored him. "Uncle Bryn? What's wrong? Why can't you speak?"

But Jackson's voice was drowned out by the rumble of an engine. An ice cream truck sled pulled up. The back doors clunked open and Uncle Bryn and his friends clambered in.

"Hey!" Jackson called. "Where are you going?"

But the truck sled had already zoomed off.

"I just don't get it," Jackson said, bouncing his flipper ball off his bedroom wall a few hours later. He and Quigley were supposed to be doing their homework project—the *Visitor's Guide to Rookeryville*—but Jackson couldn't concentrate. "I mean, why didn't Uncle Bryn tell us where he was going?"

Quigley looked up from his icePad. "Yeah, that *was* odd. He's usually quite a chatty penguin." Quigley glanced back at his screen. "Hey, do you think it's okay for us to use this photo of the Toothfish stadium? I found it on the Ice-net." He held up the screen for Jackson to see. "I know we're supposed to take our own photos, but—"

"Uncle Bryn *never* ignores me," Jackson interrupted, bouncing and catching the ball again.

"I know, right?" Quigley tapped his icePad screen some more. "Maybe this one is better," he said, showing Jackson another photo. "It's a bit blurry, so it looks like we *could* have taken it."

"And remember that freaky ice cream they were eating?" Jackson said, throwing the ball again. "Yellow and green stripes. It sort of—"

"Glowed!" Quigley looked up. "Yeah, it looked a lot like the new pajamas I invented. Did I tell you about them? They glow in the dark, so if you need a snack during the night, you can find your way. Cool, huh?"

"And why did Uncle Bryn and his friends get into that freaky-looking ice cream truck sled?" Jackson said. "Did you see it? Blacked-out windows. Yellow stripes down the side! I've never seen that truck selling ice cream in Rookeryville before, have you?"

Quigley shook his head. "Hey, do you want to use this picture of the department store where your mom works?" He held the icePad up again. "Waddles' has got to be a top place to include in a visitor's guide to Rookeryville, right?"

Jackson stopped bouncing his ball. "Maybe it wasn't an ice cream truck sled at all. Maybe it was an FBI vehicle. Maybe Uncle Bryn and his friends were just going off on a secret mission." Jackson sighed. "But that still doesn't explain why he wouldn't talk to me. He was like a zombie. Did you see his eyes? All round and staring and—"

"Maybe they were on a stakeout?" Quigley suggested.

"At Brain Freezers?" Jackson paused. Then he nodded slowly. "Yeah, maybe that's it. Uncle Bryn couldn't speak to me because he was trying to blend in. But I still don't—"

"Hey, hatchlings!" The bedroom door opened a crack and the head of Jackson's sister, Finola, appeared around the side. "Mom says stop banging your ball against the wall or she'll put you back on poop-scooping duty!" Finola sniggered.

Jackson tossed the flipper ball at her, but quick as lightning she pulled a large drumstick out of her crest and smacked the ball right back at him. Jackson ducked as it whizzed across the room and *thwump*ed into the wall, making a hole.

"Uh-oh!" Quigley gulped. "Your mom will go Hammerhead when she sees that hole."

"Nah," Jackson said. "Dad's knocking down that wall next week to build my new circus-skills training area."

"Circus skills?" Quigley's eyes widened.

"Yep. Trampoline. Trapeze. And a real tight-rope!" Jackson grinned. "Every secret agent needs good balancing skills, right?"

Finola snorted. "I always thought you clowns belonged in a circus! Mom says there are hot krill cakes in the kitchen if you want some. But maybe I'll just tell her you're too busy for cakes." She slammed the door before Jackson could chuck the ball again.

"I wish I knew what secret mission Uncle Bryn is working on," Jackson said as he and Quigley padded to the kitchen to get some food.

"Yeah, he should have let us help," Quigley said. "After all, we were the ones who cracked the case of the missing fish and got Coldfinger arrested and—"

"Shush!" Jackson nudged him as his mom shuffled into the kitchen behind them.

"How is the homework project coming?" she asked, her eyes boring into them.

"Umm, well, to be honest, not too great," Quigley began, his face turning frostberry red.

Jackson glared at him. Quigley had forgotten their new rule: Quigley was NOT allowed to talk to Jackson's mom because he wasn't able to fib to her. Jackson's mom was a detective at Waddles' Department Store, and she noticed *everything*! Jackson suspected she might be part cyborg. She definitely had honesty magnets in her eyes. No one could lie to Marina Rockflopper.

"Well, we're still in the planning stage,"

Jackson said, stepping in front of Quigley so his mom couldn't see him. "Oh, wow, those krill cakes look great."

"Oh, yeah," Quigley said. "Your dad makes THE best krill cakes on the planet."

Jackson's mom nodded. "He sure does. I just wish he'd make more cakes and fewer rooms. Lundy!" she shouted. "Come eat some of your cakes!" Then she dropped her voice and whispered to the boys, "He's in the juicing room again. I wish he wouldn't take the Egg in there with him. It nearly fell in the blender yesterday."

"Hi! Look what I made!" Jackson's dad appeared with the Egg—Jackson's soon-to-be-sibling—balanced on his toes. In his flippers he carried a giant jug of foamy green juice. "Fungi and Seaberry Smoothie! Who wants some?"

"It looks great, Mr. Rockflopper," Quigley said. "I'm in!"

"It's even better with a krill cake dipped in it." Jackson's dad picked up some cups and began to pour. "Don't you think so, Marina?"

But Jackson's mom was standing rock-still, staring at the kitchen TV. "Why is Uncle Bryn on the television?" she said, grabbing the remote so she could turn up the sound.

"Police say the alarm at Blubbers Bank went off around six o'clock this evening," the TV news anchor was saying, "when a gang of penguins broke in and stole everything in the bank's vaults. One of the intruders was caught on the security cameras making his getaway. Police say if you recognize this penguin, you should not approach him, as he may be dangerous."

"Oh, my giddy beak!" Jackson's mom collapsed onto a chair. "They're saying your uncle Bryn's a bank robber!"

"Impossible!" Jackson exploded. "Uncle Bryn's a hero, not a bank robber."

Mom grabbed her icePhone. "There must be some mistake. I'll call him. He's going to be so mad at those TV penguins."

"I'm sure I read somewhere that everyone has a doppel-penguin," Jackson's dad said, taking a large slurp of his smoothie and leaving a green mustache above his beak.

"Oh, yeah, a doppel-penguin—that's a look-alike, right?" Quigley said. "I heard that we could all have a dozen penguins who look exactly like us. Imagine!"

Jackson's head was suddenly full of a dozen Hoff Rockfaces. He shuddered.

"No reply." Mom sighed. "Bryn always forgets to turn the sound up on his cell. Let's go over there, Lundy. He'll be so embarrassed about this."

"Good plan," Jackson said. "Me and Quigley will wait in the ice sled while you get ready."

"What?" His mom frowned. "No, Jackson. You boys aren't coming. Quigley's got to go home soon. Until then, Finola will babysit."

"No, she won't!" Finola shuffled into the kitchen with her bag slung across her shoulder. "I've got band practice, remember?" Finola played drums in a heavy metal rock band called the Ice Maidens. "We've got a gig on Saturday. I'm not missing band practice to look after hatchlings."

"Don't call us that!" Jackson glared at her.

Quigley's flipper shot up, like he was answering a question in school. "Um—Jackson can come stay at my house," he said. "For a sleepover."

Jackson's mom's eyes narrowed. "But you're both grounded as part of your punishment. No sleepovers, remember?"

Jackson crossed his flippers. "Please, Mom?"

"It's not a bad idea," Jackson's dad said, picking up the ice sled keys. "We could drop them off on the way to Bryn's apartment."

Jackson's mom puffed out her cheeks. Then she sighed. "Okay. I guess I don't have a choice. I'll text your mom, Quigley, to check that it's okay; Jackson, go pack."

"I can't believe they showed Uncle Bryn's face on TV," Jackson said, throwing a few random things into his backpack. "He should make them broadcast an apology or something."

"Don't worry," Quigley said. "The FBI will know who the real robbers are."

Jackson froze. "Of course!" he said. "The FBI! You're a genius, Quigley."

"I am?"

Jackson reached under his mattress and pulled something out. "Gotcha!"

"Your uncle Bryn's FBI radio!" Quigley smiled. "I'd forgotten we still had that."

They'd found it a few weeks before, when Uncle Bryn had accidentally dropped it in one of the ponds at the aquarium. Jackson had meant to return the radio to him. But somehow he'd never gotten around to it.

"Wish they wouldn't keep changing the frequency." Jackson twiddled the knobs on the front. "Oh, here, I think I found it. Listen, they're transmitting . . ."

Calling all agents!
Calling all agents! We have a positive ID on the suspect for the Blubbers Bank job. It is FBI agent Bryn Rockflopper. Repeat, the suspect is FBI agent Bryn Rockflopper. Approach with caution.

"What?" Jackson gasped. "No way!"

"The FBI must be confused, too," Quigley said. "I mean, that bank robber on the security camera footage did look a lot like your uncle Bryn."

"We've got to go tell them," Jackson said. "They can't say that about Uncle Bryn. He's their best agent." Jackson shoved the radio into his backpack. "As soon as we get dropped off at your house, we'll sneak down to the FBI headquarters and set things straight."

Quigley nodded. "But do you think the FBI will listen? The boss isn't the friendliest penguin on the planet."

"We'll make them listen!" Jackson said. "Uncle Bryn is NOT a bank robber. It's impossible!"

They sat in silence as Jackson's parents drove the boys the two blocks to Quigley's house.

Jackson's dad tried to cheer everyone up. "You know, Bryn is going to laugh his beak off when he hears about this. Imagine having a bank robber as your double! It's like that book we read at school, Marina," he said to Jackson's mom. "*The Prince and the Pauper Penguin*! Remember? When the prince penguin swapped places with the poor penguin because they looked alike."

Mom nodded, but she still looked worried. "Please thank your mom again for me, Quigley," she said, pulling up outside his house. "I'll call in the morning. Night, honey." She smiled at Jackson. "And be good!"

"Tell Uncle Bryn I say hi," Jackson called as the sled drove off. Then he turned to Quigley. "Right! Let's do this! We've got to get down there and tell the FBI they've got it all wrong."

"Sure," Quigley said. "But first we'll have to give my mom the slip. Come on, she'll be in the shed."

Jackson followed his buddy up the overgrown drive, glancing around in case anything unexpected happened. Last week, he'd gone over to see Quigley, and the door had been answered by the vacuum cleaner—or, the Helpful House-bot, as Quigley called it. Jackson hadn't found it at all helpful. Not when it had started giving him a thorough cleaning using its extra-strong dirt-sucker! Jackson still had two bald patches as a result.

When they reached the shed, there was a loud *BANG*! The glass in the windows rattled, the door crashed open, and a thick white cloud floated out toward them.

"What the— Hey!" Jackson squeaked as it swallowed them up. "I can't see!"

"Don't worry," Quigley called out. "It's just Mom's new chemistry project, clouds in a can! It'll clear soon."

Jackson batted his way free, shaking his feathers dry. "Why would you want to put clouds in a can?"

Quigley shrugged. "To help gardeners water their plants? I dunno, really. It's Mom's project."

"Oh, hi, boys." Quigley's mom emerged from the shed wearing safety goggles and a lab coat. "Sorry about the mist." She wafted the last of the cloud away with her flipper. "It's supposed to be a rain cloud. But I can't quite get the formulation right. Nice to see you, Jackson."

"Hi, Mrs. Puffle-Popper. Mom says thanks for having me."

"Oh, it's a pleasure. Just give me five minutes to finish up and I'll come make you some snacks."

Jackson nudged Quigley. *Escape plan?* he mouthed.

"Oh—yeah, um . . ." Quigley hopped from one foot to the other. He was terrible at telling fibs. "About those snacks, Mom," he said. "I'm not sure we have any left. See, me and Dad sort of scarfed down everything in the snack cupboard last night when we were watching the flipper ball game."

"You did?" Quigley's mom sighed. "Well, Arnold does like to snack. He gets all his best ideas when he snacks."

Jackson tried not to smile. Quigley's dad, like the rest of Quigley's family, had at least twenty new invention ideas every day. Some of them were even slightly sensible. "Um, maybe we could go to the store and fetch some snacks," Jackson suggested. On a one to ten Mom Scale of Believable Ideas, it was about a two, Jackson thought, but as he watched Mrs. Puffle-Popper nodding happily at the plan, he remembered that not all moms used the same scale as his did.

"Great idea," Quigley's mom said, rummaging in her lab coat pocket. "Here, take my wallet. And, Jackson, you can borrow my ice cycle. Don't rush. I'll just carry on in here for a while. See you soon." And she shuffled back into her shed.

"I always forget how chill your mom is," Jackson said as they headed to the garage to fetch the ice cycles.

"She just likes spending time in her shed," Quigley said. "When she's in there, time stands still for her. Sometimes I go down for breakfast and she's still out in the shed from the night before."

"Is it this one?" Jackson asked, picking up an orange ice cycle inside the garage. "Yep, I can just about reach the pedals." As he steered it toward the door, he heard a crackling in his backpack. "Listen, it's the radio again." He pulled it out and turned up the volume.

**Calling all agents,
calling all agents: An intruder alarm has gone off at Diamond Feathers, the jeweler on Adele Avenue. We have reports of a robbery in progress and a sighting of rogue agent Bryn Rockflopper.
All agents respond.**

"Adele Avenue?" Jackson frowned. "Isn't that a few blocks from here? If we hurry, we could get there before the FBI—"

"—and catch the robbers!" Quigley grinned. "And prove Uncle Bryn's innocent!"

Jackson pedaled down the drive with Quigley close behind. *Don't worry, Uncle Bryn,* he thought. *No way will I let you take the blame for someone else's bad behavior! You can depend on me . . .*

"I know a shortcut," Quigley shouted as they zoomed down the now-dark street, his ice cycle light showing the way. "Follow me!"

Jackson hoped it was true. Not all of Quigley's shortcuts worked out for the best. Like the time when he'd shown Jackson a new path he'd discovered up Frostbite Ridge, the giant iceberg that loomed over Rookeryville. Halfway along, Quigley had nearly fallen into the biggest ice hole they'd ever seen. Luckily, Jackson had been able to grab his tail and pull him back from the brink. He'd only lost a few feathers, but it had been a close one. *I do not want to have to haul my buddy's butt out of a hole again tonight,* Jackson thought as they turned right, then took a hard left down a bumpy track between two houses.

"Duck!" Quigley called as they entered a tunnel of low-hanging tree branches. Seconds later they crashed through some sharp bushes and onto Adele Avenue.

"Over there!" Jackson said, spotting a flashing alarm on the front of a store halfway down the street. As they whizzed toward it, they had to swerve to avoid a truck sled thundering past.

"Hey—that's the ice cream truck sled from earlier," Jackson said.

They watched it skid to a halt outside the jewelry store just as the front doors crashed open.

Jackson felt his feathers stand on end. *No, it can't be . . .*

Quigley leaned forward. "It's hard to say for sure, what with the caps they're all wearing, but that looks an awful lot like your uncle Bryn and his friends from Brain Freezers."

Jackson had abandoned his ice cycle and was dashing across the road toward the penguins. "UNCLE BRYN! UNCLE BRYN!" He

dived between his uncle and the ice cream truck sled. "Stop! What are you doing?"

"Stand aside!" Uncle Bryn said in a robot-like voice.

"But it's me. Jackson." He reached out to grab his uncle's flipper to stop him from leaving.

But Uncle Bryn barged past him, knocking Jackson over with the large lumpy bag he was carrying on his back. He clambered into the rear of the truck sled with his friends. A heartbeat later, they were gone.

"FREEZE!" a piercing voice shouted. "Put your flippers in the air and move away from the store!" A dozen flashlights lit up Jackson's face, making him blink from their brightness. He had been too stunned by Uncle Bryn's behavior to notice the black sleds pulling up and the group of serious-looking penguins in dark glasses jumping out of them. Now, he was surrounded.

"I said, MOVE AWAY FROM THE STORE!" the voice shouted again. Then "Oh, wait—I think it's just a kid." A tall penguin wearing an FBI badge stepped forward, holding a pair of flipper-cuffs and a giant flashlight. She pointed it down into Jackson's face. "Oh, no, not you again! What on earth are you doing here? Don't tell me you're in your uncle's gang. Has he got you working as a lookout or something? Answer me!"

But Jackson couldn't speak. He just sat there on the sidewalk, his beak open and his feathers standing on end, still too shocked to say a word. *Uncle Bryn is a criminal! How can that be? It is . . . impossible!*

"Hi, Senior Agent Frost-Flipper," Quigley squeaked, appearing at Jackson's side. "We were just out late-night shopping when we saw the alarm go off at the jeweler's, so we thought we'd check it out and—"

"Does your mom know you're here?" Senior Agent Frost-Flipper interrupted, prodding Jackson.

At the word *mom*, Jackson was snapped out of his shock. He jumped up, blinking at his uncle's boss. "Um—not exactly." He gulped. Then he took a deep breath. "Uncle Bryn's innocent!" he blurted out. "He's got to be. No way would he rob a jewelry store. Or a bank." He felt his eyes prickle and looked away so the FBI boss wouldn't see. According to the secret-agent handbook (which Jackson had borrowed from Uncle Bryn and forgotten to return), secret agents never cried. Not even when their favorite heroes turned out to be the worst sort of lowdown, bank-robbing, turncoat super baddies.

Senior Agent Frost-Flipper puffed out her cheeks. She waved to her colleagues. "All right, guys, move into the store and see what they took. Don't forget to dust for flipper prints." She looked back at Jackson. "I must admit, I'm surprised at your uncle. I mean, he was never the best agent on the force—"

Jackson winced. "Hey," he began. "That's not true—"

"In fact, he was a terrible agent!" Senior Agent Frost-Flipper said. "But a bank robber? It's hard to believe."

"It's got to be a mistake," Jackson said. "Maybe it's just a penguin who looks a lot like him?"

Senior Agent Frost-Flipper shook her head. "We got flipper prints from the bank job. It's definitely him."

"Then someone's forcing him to do it!" Jackson snapped.

"Yeah, perhaps they're blackmailing him," Quigley added. "Maybe they know a secret about him—something *really* bad that they say they'll tell unless he works for them."

"A bad secret, eh?" Senior Agent Frost-Flipper rolled her eyes. "What, like the fact that he's actually a secret bank robber? Take my advice, kids. Go home and keep your beaks out of FBI business." She turned away.

"Wait—" Jackson grabbed her flipper. "See, there was this ice cream truck sled. A really weird-looking one, and Uncle Bryn got into it."

"Yeah," Quigley added. "And he was eating this strange ice cream earlier. It was so freaky. Like alien ice cream. It kind of glowed."

"I'm not interested in your uncle's snacks!" Senior Agent Frost-Flipper shook Jackson's flipper away. "Go home before I call your moms."

"But Uncle Bryn's innocent!" Jackson shouted. "I can feel it in my feathers. You've got to check out the ice cream and—"

"I'm dialing!" Senior Agent Frost-Flipper waggled her icePhone at them. "Your mom gave me her number, Jackson. One more tap and she'll be down here before you can say *grounded*!"

"Okay, okay!" Jackson backed away. "We're leaving." *But this isn't over,* he thought to himself. *Uncle Bryn's innocent, and I'm going to prove it!*

"Good morn-ing, Jack-son," said a high- pitched robot voice. "Time for a clean!"

Huh? Jackson sat bolt upright and banged his head on the bunk bed above him. "What? No! Get off!" He tried to wriggle his foot away. But the vacuum cleaner house-bot had suckered onto him. "QUIGLEY!"

His buddy's face appeared, upside down, from the bunk above. "It's okay. It's just dusting you."

"Why doesn't it dust *you?*" Jackson used both flippers to tug the bot's sucker pipe off his foot, then pulled himself up onto Quigley's bunk, out of its reach.

"I programmed it to recognize my family's DNA," Quigley explained. "Anything else that comes into the house is alien. So it cleans it up. It just thinks you're a—"

"—giant alien dirtbag!" Jackson rolled his eyes. "Great! Well, please, can you call it off? We've got work to do."

Jackson had spent most of the night lying awake, thinking up ways to prove Uncle Bryn's innocence. There was just one teeny-weeny feather-size problem. Uncle Bryn *wasn't* innocent! They'd seen him do it. They'd seen him hopping out of that jeweler's shop with what looked like a large bag of stolen gems on his back. And by now the FBI would have the flipper-prints to prove it!

"So that means there's only one explanation," Jackson told Quigley as they headed into the kitchen for breakfast. "Uncle Bryn must have been hypnotized."

Quigley nodded. "Oh, yeah, that makes sense. Hypnotism is a powerful weapon. My nana got hypnotized once to stop her snoring. It didn't work. But she could suddenly do amazing cartwheels— Watch it!" Quigley dragged Jackson down to the floor. "The dishflipper is on a countdown."

"Huh?" Jackson glanced up at the dishflipper's clock: 5, 4, 3, 2. "Uh-oh!" He ducked just in time as the dishflipper door clunked open and its entire contents—freshly washed cups, plates, bowls, knives, and other utensils—were flung out. They shot across the kitchen toward a huge, rubbery shelving unit, where they landed with a *thwump*!

"Bravo!" Quigley's dad cheered as he shuffled into the kitchen. "Looks like only two cups broken today. You've done a great job improving it, son."

Quigley beamed.

Jackson wanted to ask why they didn't just empty their dishflipper themselves, like regular penguins. But he knew never to question the gadget-loving Puffle-Popper family.

"Morning, all!" Mrs. Puffle-Popper shuffled in, scooping up a cap from the kitchen counter. As she put it on, a crab claw popped out of the side of the hat and dangled down around her face as a mouthpiece for her to speak into. "Coffeepot ON!" she said into the mouthpiece, and Jackson heard a click on the counter as the coffeepot responded.

Quigley nudged him. "It's one of Sunny's caps. Remember?"

Jackson nodded. They'd seen Quigley's cousin with a similar hat a few weeks earlier. Jackson remembered how much Quigley had admired it.

"Pancake machine ON!" Mrs. Puffle-Popper said, and a grill on the counter lit up. "Oh, Jackson, your mom just called," she said, moving the crab-claw mouthpiece to the side. "She says there's been a small mix-up concerning your uncle. But you're not to worry. They just haven't managed to speak to him yet, to sort it all out."

Jackson's shoulders drooped. *How could*

they speak to him, when Uncle Bryn's probably hiding out somewhere in his ice cream truck sled getaway vehicle!

"Your parents are seeing your uncle's boss when your mom gets off work," she went on. "I said you could spend the day with us until they're finished."

"Thanks." Jackson glanced over at Quigley. No way were they staying at Quigley's house. Not when they had to find out who had hypnotized Uncle Bryn.

"Pancakes are ready!" Mrs. Puffle-Popper called. "Plates!"

The pancakes pinged out of the machine and were now flying through the air, heading for the table. Jackson knew he was supposed to hold out his plate, because the sensors in his seat were supposed to tell the pancake machine that a penguin was sitting there and needed a pancake deposited on its plate. But he'd gotten biffed in the beak every time he ate at the Puffle-Poppers, so now Jackson had a new method—the use-your-plate-as-a-shield method.

It worked. *Splat!* His pancake hit the plate instead of his face. Jackson lowered the plate and—*splat!* A second pancake smacked him in the beak.

"Oh, sorry, Jackson," Mrs. Puffle-Popper said. "The pancake machine is doing doubles again. So, what have you boys got planned for today?"

"Um—homework." Jackson scraped the pancake off his beak and glanced at Quigley. No way could they tell his mom about their secret mission to clear Uncle Bryn's name.

"We're making a *Visitor's Guide to Rookeryville,*" Quigley explained. "We've got to go take pictures of all the famous landmarks in town."

"You should stop by my garage," Mr. Puffle-Popper said. "It's a landmark!"

Mrs. Puffle-Popper smiled. "Sure is, honey."

Mr. Puffle-Popper puffed out his chest with pride. "I could show you kids the new gear system Sunny and I have come up with." As well as fixing fairground rides on the pier, Sunny often helped out in Quigley's dad's garage.

"Cool!" Quigley breathed. "What does the gear system do, Dad?"

Jackson checked the time on his wrist-flipper. *Oh, man! We don't have time for this. We have to get going!*

"Well, we call it the hopper gear," Mr. Puffle-Popper waffled on. "It makes a sled hop over any holdups, like traffic jams or snowdrifts, or wandering walruses." He smiled. "We've just fitted it to a fleet of ice cream truck sleds, along with rocket boosters and—"

"Huh?" Jackson nearly choked on his pancake. "Ice cream truck sleds?"

Mr. Puffle-Popper took a last slurp of juice and picked up his keys. "Yep, ice cream truck sleds! A bit strange. You'd think they'd want their ice cream truck sleds to go slowly, not fast! Otherwise, how can people stop them to buy an ice cream?"

Jackson felt his feathers stand on end. His danger detectors were sounding. "Um, Mr. Puffle-Popper, who owns the ice cream truck sleds?" *Please don't say Bryn Rockflopper,* he thought, crossing his flippers.

"Oh, it's one of Sunny's customers." Mr. Puffle-Popper scratched his crest. "I can't remember the name. Anyway, I've got to hop. So long, boys. Have a great day."

Big Bong, the giant Rookeryville Frost clock, was chiming ten as Jackson and Quigley whizzed past on their way to Brain Freezers.

"I just don't get it!" Jackson shouted. "Why would an ice cream truck sled need rocket boosters and a hopping gear?"

Quigley nodded. "It doesn't make sense."

"Unless"—Jackson frowned—"unless the ice cream truck sled is really a bank-robbing, jewel-thieving getaway vehicle!"

They skidded to a halt outside Brain Freezers.

"I wish my dad could remember who owns the truck sleds," Quigley said. "Maybe we could go ask Sunny?"

"Good plan. We'll go find him after we've checked out Brain Freezers." Jackson headed for the door. "This is where the whole mix-up started. There's got to be a clue in here somewhere."

As they walked in, Quigley nudged Jackson. "Victor's back!" He waved to a round-faced penguin with a heavily gelled crest who was standing behind the counter.

"Quigley! Jackson!" Victor smiled. "*Ice* to see you! The usual?"

"Sure, thanks," Jackson said.

"I'll bring them over." Victor reached for the shake glasses while Jackson and Quigley made their way to their favorite booth.

"Nothing!" Jackson said, after checking around the seats and looking under the table. He wasn't sure what he'd been hoping to find, but a leaflet advertising an evil criminal hypnotist would have been a good start.

"Here you go." Victor appeared with a tray. "Two frostberry-seaweed specials, shaken not stirred." When he leaned over to place their drinks on the table, Jackson noticed a gold medal pinned to his apron.

"What's that, Victor?" he asked.

"Real fancy, isn't it!" Victor puffed out his chest. "We won it in the best café contest!"

Quigley took a slurp of his shake. "Mmm, you definitely deserve that medal."

Victor blushed. "Aw, thanks. That's why we were closed yesterday; we were at the awards ceremony."

Jackson frowned. "But you weren't closed yesterday. We were here."

"Hey!" Victor had turned to glare at a group of rowdy young penguins playing flipper ball with a rolled-up napkin on the other side of the café. "Stop that!"

"It's Hoff Rockface and his buddies," Quigley whispered to Jackson.

"So rude!" Victor sighed. "Can I get you anything else? Did I mention about our new ice cream?" He passed them each a menu. "They're *real* fancy! They're made by Frosters."

"Frosters?" Jackson hadn't heard of that brand before.

"Oh yeah, it's this fancy new ice cream factory down by the docks."

Jackson smiled. *Fancy* was Victor's favorite word.

Victor pointed to his medal. "That's where the awards ceremony was held. They gave us a tour and let us taste a whole bunch of exotic ice cream. They sure do make some fancy flavors in that factory!"

"Wait—" Jackson frowned. A tiny alarm was sounding in the back of his brain. *Fancy flavors?* "Um—do they make a green-and-yellow-striped ice cream that kind of glows?"

Victor chuckled. "Glows? Ha! Good one, Jackson. Nope, I didn't see any glowing ice cream. But I did pick up a tub of some lovely pink sorbet called Freezy-Breezy Lemon Squeezy. It's real fancy. Want to try some?"

Before Jackson could answer, there was a loud *SMASH!* from Hoff's direction.

"Oh, my feathers!" Victor gasped. "That's another glass gone! Sorry, boys, I have to go fetch a brush and pan. Have an ICE day!"

"Did you hear that?" Jackson whispered as soon as Victor had gone. "About the fancy flavors at that ice cream factory? What was it called—Frosters, was it? Maybe that's where the weird ice cream Uncle Bryn was eating came from."

Quigley nodded. "And why did Victor say they were closed yesterday?"

"Yeah, I wondered about that, too. Maybe he just got his days muddled. Or maybe—" Jackson shivered. "Something odd is happening here," he said, glancing around the diner. "I can feel it in my feathers."

"Surely you don't think Victor's involved?" Quigley shook his head. "He's the last penguin on the planet who would get mixed up in bank robbing."

Jackson sighed. "I thought that about Uncle Bryn, too, and look what's happened to him." He glanced up at one of Victor's employees who was waddling past with a large bag of trash. Something at the bottom of it caught Jackson's eye. "Quigley!" he hissed. "I swear I saw something glowing in that trash bag. Come on, we've got to go check it out."

They left some coins for their drinks on the table and slipped past Victor, who was crouched on the floor, sweeping up the glass by Hoff's table. They followed the employee through the back and outside to the dumpsters, hiding behind a pile of crates as the worker deposited the sack and went back inside.

"Come on, let's take a look." Jackson led the way. He flipped open the dumpster lid and both penguins stood on tiptoes to peer inside.

"There!" Jackson said. "The ice cream carton at the bottom of that bag."

"Try and grab it," Quigley said. "If there's enough ice cream left inside, we can take it back to my mom's lab and run some tests."

Jackson leaned in as far as he dared. But just then— "Hey!" He felt a sudden, hard shove in his back. And— "Whoa! I'm falling!"— Jackson's beak hit the trash bags. Quigley landed on top of him. And they heard a familiar, annoying laugh from above. "So long, losers!" a voice said, and then everything went black.

"Hoff Rockface!" Jackson growled in the darkness. "I'd know that voice anywhere! He must have followed us outside." The boys heard a lock snap shut. Jackson pummeled the lid of the dumpster. "LET US OUT! LET US OUT!"

"Sorry, loser patrol!" Hoff shouted. "Trash belongs in a dumpster! Ha-ha!"

"Grrrr!" Jackson flopped back down onto the sacks. "Don't panic, Agent Q," he added. "There's got to be a way out of this—whoa!" He blinked in the beam of Quigley's flashlight.

"Such a bad design," Quigley said, examining the rim of the dumpster. "No emergency-escape release mechanism."

"I guess not many penguins get stuck inside a dumpster." Jackson frowned. "We've got to think like secret agents." He scratched his crest. "Um—maybe we could ninja kick the lock. Move over. I'll give it a try."

"Wait, I've got another idea." Quigley pulled open his backpack. "See, I've got this new gadget. I reckon it'll get us out of here before you can say 'Agent Q is a genius.'"

Jackson peered at the long, thin device Quigley was waggling. "I'm not sure a crest comb is going to help us much."

"But this is no ordinary crest comb!" Quigley flicked a switch and the teeth of the comb began to whir and rotate. "See, it works like a chainsaw." The teeth were moving faster now, their sharp points glistening in the flashlight's beam.

Jackson flattened himself against the side of the dumpster. *Whoa! Agent Q nearly took my beak off!* "Um—maybe I should hold the flashlight. I think you need both flippers for that thing."

But Quigley couldn't hear over the noise of the whirring. "Look at it go!" he shouted. "It's cutting through the lock like it's made of Jell-O."

While Quigley worked, Jackson dug around the trash bags, hoping to spot the ice cream glowing in the darkness. "Urgh," he muttered as his flippers touched something sticky. "Smells like toffee sauce!" Then, there it was. "I found it!" Jackson pulled a small tub out of the sack. A tiny trace of the ice cream that was stuck to the bottom gleamed brightly. He felt a bubble of excitement in his belly. He was about to show it to Quigley when he heard a chugging outside.

"Two more minutes," Quigley called, "and I'll have us out of here! I can see daylight now."

But daylight wasn't the only thing Jackson could see through the hole Quigley had made. "Err—you need to get a wiggle on," Jackson said, his heart starting to pound in his chest. "Because that looks a lot like the dumpster truck sled out there. I think we're about to be emptied!"

There was a loud *CLANG!* and then the rattle of chains, and their dumpster suddenly lurched one way, then the other, and began to rise.

"Just a few more seconds . . . ," Quigley said.

Jackson braced himself against one of the dumpster's sides as it lurched to a stop, dangling in midair.

"Done!" Quigley shouted, and the lid flipped open.

Jackson gasped. They were super high; at least thirty flippers off the ground. He waved to the driver. "Hey! Up here! You've got to stop!" But a moment later, he muttered, "It's no good. I don't think he can hear me over his engine."

"Have you seen that crusher?" Quigley peered over the edge and shuddered.

"Um, yeah, but don't worry," Jackson said, trying to make his buddy feel better. But inside he was quaking. *If we put one flipper in that thing we'll be mincemeat! They'll have to scoop us out and send us home in a plastic tub.*

"Quick! We'll have to jump!" Jackson started to scramble up over the side.

"Wait—put this on!" Quigley thrust something flowery into Jackson's flippers.

"What? No!" Jackson groaned. "Not the Poop Protector Hats again—"

"They've got a heli-hopper mode," Quigley said. "Just flick the switch on the top three times."

Jackson didn't argue. Their dumpster had begun to tip. He pulled on the hat, flicked the switch three times and bailed out over the side with his spoons spinning and his eyes shut. *Please don't let Hoff see me,* he thought. *He'd never let me live this down.* But then—

"Shocking squids!" Jackson breathed as he glided softly to the ground. "It works!"

"Phew!" Quigley landed next to him. "That's a relief. I'd never tested the heli-hopper mode before." He chuckled. "Good thing I didn't get it mixed up with the self-destruct mode."

"The what?" Jackson stared at Quigley.

"Didn't I tell you?" His buddy grinned. "I always add a self-destruct mode to my inventions"—he turned off their hats with a small remote control unit—"in case they fall into enemy hands. We wouldn't want that, now, would we?"

Jackson shuddered. "I guess not. Come on," he said, "let's get out of here before that truck sled drops the dumpster on our heads."

They headed for the alleyway, running along the side of Brain Freezers.

"At least we got the carton." Jackson stopped for a moment and held it up so Quigley could see the tiny trace of yellow-and-green ice cream still glowing at the bottom.

Quigley frowned. “I’m not sure there’s enough for me to analyze. I guess we could go try.”

Jackson didn’t answer. He was peering at a label on the side of the tub. “I’ve got another idea. Look . . . there’s a manufacturer’s name at the bottom.”

“Frosters?” Quigley read.

“Yep, Frosters!” Jackson’s eyes narrowed. “The same factory that held the awards ceremony yesterday, where Victor and his team went. Remember, Victor said the café was closed. And he probably thought it was. But we know it wasn't!" He scratched his crest and tried to order the facts in his brain. "Maybe someone just wanted to get Victor and his staff out of the way so they could use his café for something else."

"Like hypnotizing your uncle Bryn?" Quigley nodded. "Wow! Sneaky trick. And you think someone at Frosters might be involved?"

Jackson shrugged. "I don't know, but I think we need to check this Frosters factory out. Look—there's an address on the label: Unit Thirteen, Driftwood Docks, Rookeryville."

"That's not far from here," Quigley said. "And I just thought of something else. Maybe Frosters has its own fleet of ice cream truck sleds!"

"Hmm . . ." Jackson nodded slowly, a new thought crystallizing in his brain. *And maybe Frosters' ice cream trucks sleds have rocket boosters on the back and hopper gears.* "Like the ones your dad has been working on," he said aloud.

Quigley nodded. "Exactly!" Then he sighed. "Shame we haven't got time to find Hoff Rockface. We could have been pulverized to death in that dumpster truck sled thanks to him."

"Don't worry, we'll get him back," Jackson muttered. "Finola always says 'Revenge is a dish best served cold!'"

"Huh?" Quigley scratched his crest.

"I dunno what it means, either," Jackson admitted. "But I know one thing for sure—Hoff's got a lot of credits in the Bank of Payback! And sooner or later he's going to have to make a withdrawal. Come on. We've got to clear Uncle Bryn's name. And find out who's really pulling the strings on these robberies. Let's do this!"

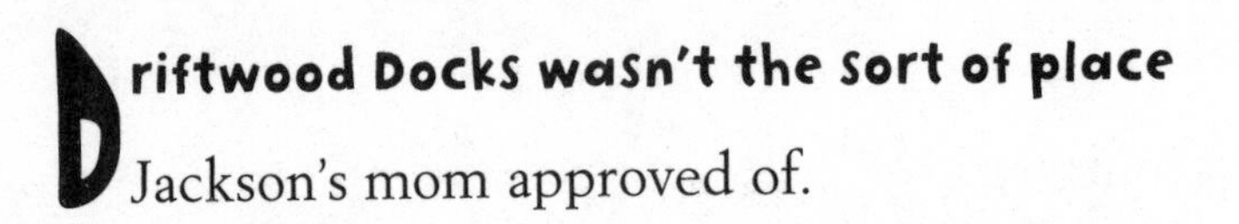

Driftwood Docks wasn't the sort of place Jackson's mom approved of.

MOM'S LIST OF PLACES JACKSON AND QUIGLEY MUST NOT VISIT—EVER!

1. Frostbite Ridge, the large iceberg above town: WAY too slippery.

2. Driftwood Docks: WAY too busy.

3. Criminal Lairs: WAY too many baddies.

4. FBI HQ: WAY too much secret-agent business for would-be junior secret agents to stick their beaks into!

"Watch it!" Jackson pulled Quigley out of the way of a reversing log-loader sled.

But Quigley didn't notice. "That's the third milk truck that's arrived in the last five minutes," he said, peering through his bin-ice-ulars at the factory across the street. "But I haven't seen any rocket-boosted ice cream truck sleds."

"Can I see?" Jackson borrowed the bin-ice-ulars and scanned the area from the delivery gates to the front entrance, where groups of penguins were lining up outside. "Looks like they have a visitor center," Jackson said. "Come on, we can get inside that way."

A small penguin with well-muscled flippers who was wearing a cap and a badge that said HI, MY NAME IS THELMA. I'M HERE TO HELP! was waving the line inside. "If everyone can please follow the blue footprints painted on the floor, then you'll be able to see the whole magical Frosters experience in complete safety," she said. "Please DO NOT detour from the blue footprints. Anyone who detours from the blue footprints will be in big trouble! I repeat, STAY ON THE BLUE FOOTPRINTS!"

Jackson and Quigley exchanged glances. *No way* were they going to stay on the blue footprints. If there was any funny business going on in the factory, they knew it wasn't going to be happening anywhere near the blue footprints!

"Mmm, smells good," Quigley said as they followed the line of visitors into a large room with several mixing vats churning sugar, seaweed, and cream. "Maybe they'll let us try some."

Jackson's tummy rumbled. It *did* smell good. But the first rule of secret-agent survival was: No snack breaks!

"Look, there's Lily from school. Hi, Lily!" Quigley waved to a girl penguin at the front of the line.

Lily had helped them on their last mission. And even though she wanted to be a rare-fish keeper at the aquarium when she grew up, just like her dad, Jackson thought she'd make a good secret agent—with a little training from him and Quigley, of course.

"Maybe we could join her group," Quigley said. "Look, I think that's what she's telling us to do. See? She's waving us over."

Jackson waved back and smiled. "Um—maybe later," he whispered. "She's with her little cousin from first grade. I think it's a birthday outing. See? The little girl's got a balloon. Do you really want to go join a hatchling's birthday party?"

Quigley winced. "Um—perhaps not."

Jackson glanced around at the workers in the room. Some were checking gauges. Others were filling out charts. Could one of them be an evil hypnotizing, bank-robbing super-criminal mastermind?

"Keep moving along the blue footprints!" shouted Thelma, the tour group leader. As they followed, she began to explain the ice cream–making process, which sounded a lot like "*Blah blah blah, KEEP FOLLOWING THE BLUE FOOTPRINTS!*" to Jackson. The other visitors nodded along, *ooh*ing and *aah*ing at the impossibly large amounts of ice cream Thelma told them Frosters made.

But Jackson had zoned out. *There has to be more to this place than meets the eye,* he thought. *I can feel it in my feathers!* And then he spotted it—a corridor leading away from the blue footprints with a sign above it saying:

He nudged Quigley, who nodded back.

"STAY ON THE BLUE FOOTPRINTS!" they heard Thelma shout from the head of the line. "WE'RE NOW GOING THROUGH TO

THE FLAVORS ROOM. DO NOT TOUCH ANYTHING! DO NOT EAT ANYTHING! STAY ON THE BLUE FOOTPRINTS!"

Jackson and Quigley waited until she wasn't looking, and then—

Now! Jackson mouthed, and they raced down the empty white-walled corridor, hearts beating fast, feathers standing on end, expecting at any moment to feel one of Thelma's well-muscled flippers hauling them back to the blue footprints. Seconds later they reached a set of double doors.

"Locked!" Jackson grimaced.

But Quigley already had his remote control out and was pointing it at a keypad to one side of the doors. "My remote's got a confuse-a-tron mode," he whispered. "It'll electronically bombard the locking system with number combinations until it malfunctions. It just needs a few seconds . . ."

Jackson glanced behind them, his tummy doing somersaults. *Were we seen? Are there any security cameras watching us? What if Thelma has already noticed we're gone and set off a silent alarm? At any moment, an army of small, well-muscled Frosters guards might appear and—*

"Bingo!" Quigley said as a green light showed on the keypad and the door clicked open.

"Awesome work," Jackson murmured as they slipped through. "Remind me to borrow that device for the new lock on Finola's secret strongbox."

Through the doors was another corridor, and at the far end, Jackson could see a cloakroom with rows of white lab coats hanging on pegs. And just beyond there was another set of doors, with glass windows. "Let's go take a look," Jackson whispered, leading the way.

They had to stand on tiptoes to peer through the glass, but then—

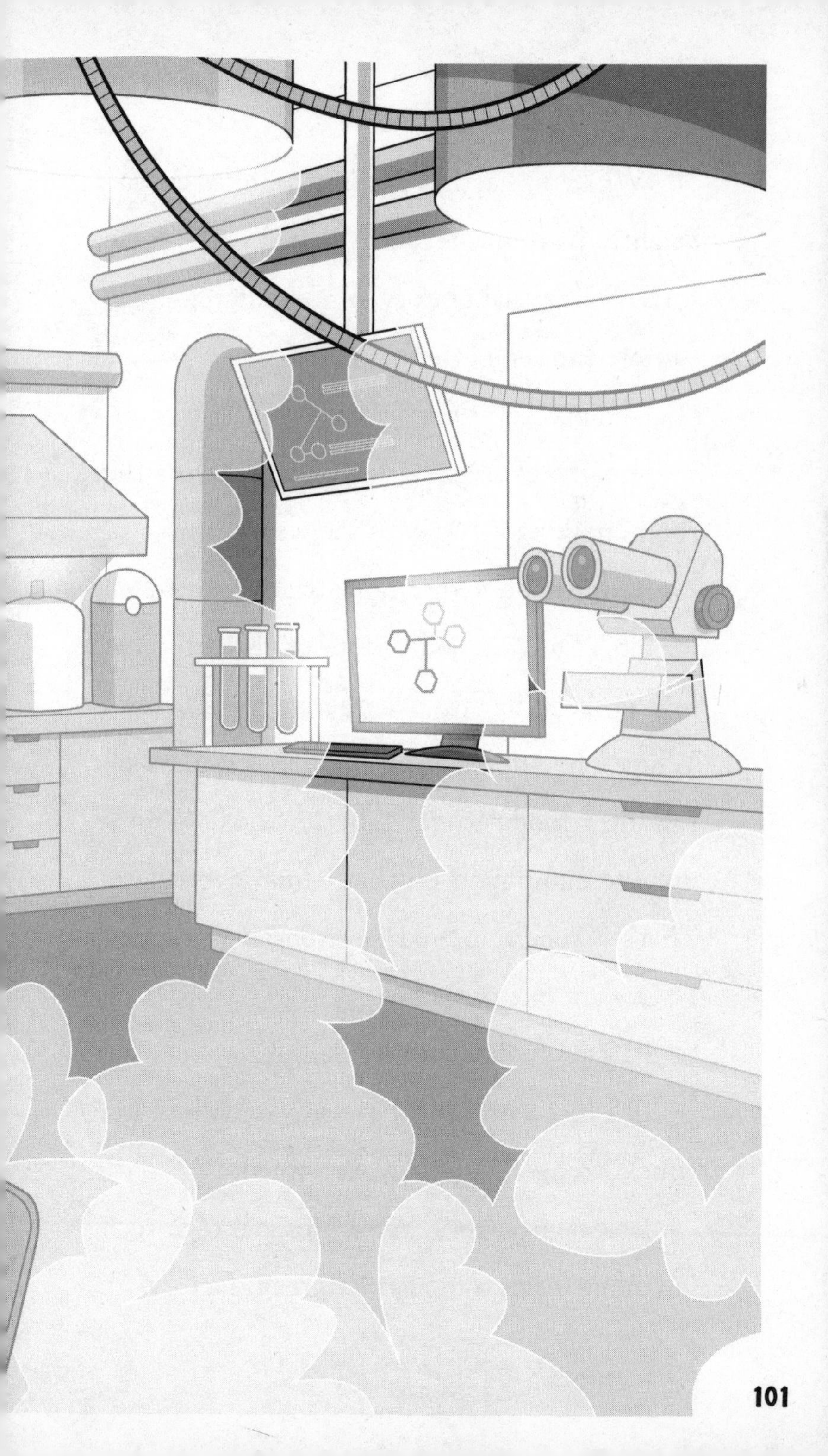

"What on earth?" Jackson blinked at the brightly lit room beyond. "It looks like some sort of crazy laboratory made out of—" He squinted to see better.

"—neon ice!" Quigley squeaked. "So cool!"

Streams of freezing fog blasted across the room, making it tricky to see clearly.

"It must be a thermostatically controlled ice lab," Quigley said. "State of the art! That fog is keeping the temperature sub-zero. Whoa!" he added, using his bin-ice-ulars on fog-filter mode to get a better look. "Check out the equipment on that bench over there. That's a super-powered electron-micro-flipper! I SO want one of those."

Jackson looked at him blankly.

"It's like a microscope—only a krill-zillion times stronger!" Quigley explained.

Jackson frowned. "What's a super high-tech lab doing inside a regular ice cream factory?"

"Dunno, but I can't wait to find out." Quigley pointed his remote control at the keypad lock on the doors.

"Wait. We should probably put these on." Jackson handed Quigley a white lab coat. "If there's anyone in there, it'll help us blend in. Look, there are goggles in the pockets." He slipped on a pair. "Tinted!" he said as the world turned yellow. "Neat!"

They slipped inside and a blast of cold air hit Jackson's face. His feathers stood on end, and he was pretty sure his lungs had just frozen solid. He shivered. Then he shivered even more because he suddenly realized the room was full of penguins. Through the blasting fog, at the far end of the neon ice room, he could see a dozen or so penguins in lab coats and goggles working at benches. And overseeing their work was a tall, scary-looking penguin with a spiked crest and razor-sharp flippers.

Jackson craned his neck to see better. *Is that a real, live gull on his flipper?* It made him look a lot like a pirate penguin. That, and the long crest braid running down his back.

Quigley nudged him. "Look at what they're making," he whispered, pointing to the work-benches. "Glowing ice cream! Just like the stuff your uncle was eating."

The scientist penguins couldn't hear Quigley over the noise of the cold-air blasters, but the gull sitting on the pirate penguin's flipper suddenly turned its head and stared at them. *Uh-oh,* Jackson thought, trying not to move in case he startled the bird. *I don't think that gull likes the look of us.* He was about to warn Quigley when—

"SQUAWK!" The gull let out a shriek, and all heads turned to see what had happened.

Jackson tugged Quigley behind a cart of chemicals just in time. "We've got to distract that bird so we can get our flippers on some of that ice cream."

"Wait—I know . . ." Quigley rummaged in his backpack and pulled out the silent gull whistle Jackson had blown on Mrs. Hoppy-Floppy's deck. He took a deep breath and blew.

The effect was instantaneous!

The seagull fluttered its feathers. It squawked, then took off, flapping up into the air, then swooping and diving around the room.

"Fluffy!" boomed the pirate penguin. "Stop that at once!"

Fluffy? Jackson mouthed to Quigley.

Quigley smiled, then blew the whistle some more.

"Stop your work!" the pirate penguin shouted to the other penguins. "Help me catch Fluffy!"

"Fluffy! Fluffy! Here, Fluffy!" As the scientist penguins tried to catch the bird, Jackson dropped to the floor and began crawling across the lab underneath the workbenches. *It's like being in a maze in the fog,* he thought. *I just need to remember which bench has the ice cream on it.* He popped his head up seal-at-an-ice-hole-style. *There: two benches to the right.* He dropped down again and crawled a bit farther before popping up once more. Several tubs of glowing ice cream lay on the bench in front of him. But as Jackson reached out a flipper, the pirate penguin turned around.

Slithering spikefish! Jackson froze. *I've been spotted!*

Jackson stared across the room through the wispy cold fog, straight into the icy face of the pirate penguin; his small, evil-looking eyes glared through his goggles.

Uh-oh! Jackson felt his feathers stiffen; his danger detectors were maxing out at 10. *Do*

something, 00Zero! he told himself. *Quick!* "Um—Fluffy!" he found himself shouting, his voice high and wobbly. "Here, Fluffy! Come back now!" He waggled his flippers at the swooping bird just like the other scientists were doing. The pirate penguin stared at him, uncertainty washing over his face.

Jackson held his breath. He was banking on the fact that through the fog, and in his lab coat and goggles, he looked a lot like the other penguins in the room, only shorter. "Fluffy! Fluffy!" he called again. "Whoa!" He ducked as the gull dived down from the ceiling, nearly taking his crest off, and then swooped away again. The pirate penguin made a grab for his bird, tripping and stumbling over a high stool. As he hit the floor, Jackson seized his chance. He swiped a tub of ice cream and fled.

Run! he mouthed to Quigley, who already had the doors open.

"Did he see you take it?" Quigley whispered.

"I don't know," Jackson muttered. "But we'd better get out of here fast. This way," he said, heading for another door off the corridor. "Flippers crossed it's a quick exit!"

This time, luck was on their side. The doors weren't locked, and they shot straight outside, onto a metal ramp at the back of the factory.

"Keep running!" Jackson said, pushing his goggles up onto the top of his head and blinking in the sudden daylight. They shuffled down the ramp, dodging several workers pushing carts in the opposite direction, and followed the path around the side of the building.

"I guess this is the loading dock," Quigley panted as they slowed to catch their breath. "Check out the truck sleds."

To their right were dozens of trucks coming and going, turning and reversing, chugging their loads in and out of the factory gates while chunky penguins in aprons charged around, pushing enormous carts laden with boxes and churns and giant sacks of ice cream ingredients.

"I don't see the truck sled from last night," Quigley said, scanning the grounds to make sure.

Jackson glanced behind them in case they were being followed. *Phew! Nope, all clear!* Maybe they'd actually gotten away with it? He felt his feathers puff up. *This is exactly why the FBI needs us,* he thought.

"So that's the ice cream," Quigley said, peering at the tub Jackson had swiped. "Weird, isn't it? So bright, and"—he leaned in closer—"so smelly! It kind of stinks like bathroom cleaner. I can't wait to run some tests on it. But what do you think it's got to do with this whole hypnotized-uncle business?"

"I don't know. Maybe nothing but—"

"Watch it!" A large penguin pushing a cart of milk churns clattered past them.

Jackson stuffed the tub into his backpack. "Hope it doesn't melt too quickly," he whispered. "I think my spelling book is in there."

Quigley nodded. Miss Chalk-Feather would NOT approve of sticky spelling homework.

"Come on. Let's see if we can find a fast route out of here." Jackson led the way. "Hey," he called back to his buddy, "did you see that crazy-looking pirate dude in the laboratory? His eyes! Sheesh! Scare-EEE!"

"Jackson! Stop!" Quigley's face had turned pale. "Over there. Look what just pulled up."

Jackson peered over at the loading dock. A large ice cream truck sled was reversing into the loading bay. He gasped, steadying himself against the wall of the building. "Same blacked-out windows," he muttered. "Same yellow stripes."

"It's the one your uncle drove off in!" Quigley said. "I'm sure of it. Hey, maybe he's still inside!"

Jackson nodded. If Uncle Bryn *was* still inside, then this was the perfect opportunity to make him snap out of the hypnotism. Jackson had seen TV magicians do that by clicking their flippers in front of the penguins they'd hypnotized. *It's worth a try,* he thought. "Quick, let's get over there!"

The driver and his partner were already out of the truck and unlocking the back doors when Jackson and Quigley reached the loading dock.

"I don't recognize them," Jackson said, shuffling closer. "But they're wearing the same caps as Uncle Bryn had on. Look, see there, the letter *F*? It must be *F* for Frosters!"

The penguins had found a cart and were unloading a large chest freezer from the back of the truck sled onto it.

"I don't see your uncle," Quigley murmured, peering past the penguins and into the back of the truck.

Jackson looked, too. He felt a wobble of disappointment that Uncle Bryn wasn't there. "Watch it, they're coming this way," he whispered as the penguins set off with their load.

He stepped out of the way when they pushed past. But just then, one of the cart's wheels hit a stone and the freezer's lid bounced open for a moment.

Jackson gasped. "Jewels!" he muttered. "Look, it's full of sparkling jewels—"

He shut up immediately, because the smaller penguin shot him a death stare. "Shouldn't you be in the laboratory!" she said, glancing at Jackson's lab coat.

"Um . . . Well, we're on a break—" Jackson began.

"—from very important ice cream experiments!" Quigley added in a way that sounded as if he was sure it was helpful. But Jackson knew it absolutely wasn't, because both penguins had stopped pushing their cart and were staring at them.

The smaller penguin's eyes narrowed. She stepped closer and her beak piercing glistened in the sun. "Aren't you a bit young to be working here?"

Before Jackson could reply, Quigley dived in. "Oh, yes, we are young, but we're very advanced for our age. In fact, we're here on work placement, sharing our detailed knowledge of ice cream genetics." Quigley's cheeks turned shrimp pink and he swallowed several times.

Jackson cringed. He was pretty sure he'd specifically asked Quigley to leave all secret-agent undercover fibbing to him, because Quigley was sub-zero on the Secret-Agent Scale of Advanced Fibbing.

"Show me your passes!" the smaller penguin snapped.

"Err, sure," Jackson patted his lab coat pockets. "Oh, sorry, I appear to have left mine in the lab; I'll just go get it." He turned to go, signaling to Quigley to follow.

"That's the wrong way for the lab," the small penguin called. "You need to go back up the ramp. WAIT—STOP! I don't like this," she shouted. "Something stinks!"

"What, like bathroom cleaner?" Quigley turned back. "Oh, don't worry about that, I can explain the strange smell coming from Jackson's backpack, you see the ice cream has a pungent chemical aroma and—"

"It's all right," Jackson interrupted, grabbing Quigley's flipper and dragging him across the loading dock. "We don't have time to talk right now. Too many, uh, experiments to do. Catch you later."

"WAIT!" the penguin shouted again. But Jackson and Quigley were running now.

"We've got to get back inside the factory and find those blue footprints again," Jackson puffed.

"What?" Quigley couldn't believe his feathers. "You're joking! We've only just got out."

"Look around," Jackson whispered. "There's barbed wire at the tops of the fences. The only way out of this loading dock is through that gate, and I'm certain that security penguin over there is not going to let us just walk out."

Quigley glanced at a big-bellied older penguin staring over at them with suspicious eyes.

"We've got to get back on that tour," Jackson said. "Then we can leave through the front door with the other penguins. Come on, let's do this!" Jackson spotted a set of doors propped open, with several penguins pushing carts through it. "Hi," he called to one. "Which way is the visitor center? We're new here and, uh, we're supposed to be giving a talk about the science of ice cream."

"Just follow that corridor right to the end," the penguin said. "Go through a set of doors and then you'll see blue footprints on the floor. Follow the footprints to the visitor center."

"Great. Thanks! Bye!" he called to the penguin. "Hey, can you hear that alarm going off?" he muttered to Quigley. "I'm pretty sure it has something to do with us."

As they ran down the corridor, they took off their lab coats and goggles and stuffed them into their backpacks.

"Did you see the jewels in that chest?" Jackson panted.

Quigley nodded. "Yep. Now we know for sure—Frosters is involved in the robberies."

"We just need to find out how they roped in Uncle Bryn. Geez!" Jackson covered his ears with his flippers. "That alarm is spreading through the factory faster than a bad rumor in a lunch line."

Heads down, flippers waggling, Jackson and Quigley hurtled down the rest of the corridor. But before they could reach the doors at the end—

SLAM! The doors burst open in front of them and a bossy voice shouted: "Freeze, busters! You're in BIG trouble!"

Thelma, the bossy tour guide, glared at them. "What do you think you're doing?"

A tidal wave of sweat passed through Jackson's feathers. It felt a lot like being called into the principal's office. "Um—sorry," he squeaked. "We got lost."

"You betcha you did!" Thelma put her muscly flippers on her hips. "I warned you!" she said, leaning in so close that Jackson could smell her breakfast: peanut butter and smoked sardines! "I told you to STAY ON THE BLUE FOOTPRINTS!"

"We're sorry. We were just looking for the—um—bathroom." Jackson hung his head. *Is now the time to try out my fake crying skills?* he wondered. He'd been practicing the technique for weeks—secret-agent survival skill number forty-seven: how to look really sorry to elicit sympathy from your enemy. Not that this worked all the time, Jackson had discovered. He'd tried the technique on his mom two days before, when he'd used her favorite china cup in a balancing experiment that hadn't gone quite as well as he'd hoped. The fake tears had been an epic fail.

"We won't do it again," Quigley added, shuffling his feet.

"Well, all right, then," Thelma said. "I forgive you!"

"You do?" Jackson gave Quigley a sideways glance. *Surely this couldn't be that easy?* "No punishment?"

"Ha! Who do you think I am? Your mom?" Thelma laughed.

Jackson laughed nervously. Maybe she actually did know his mom!

"Follow me," Thelma said. "We're about to do the fun bit—make ice cream sundaes. But STAY ON THE BLUE FOOTPRINTS!"

They followed Thelma through the doors, down the hall, and into a large visitors' area where groups of penguins making ice cream sundaes sat around circular tables. Lily from school waved to them. Her little cousin and her cousin's friends seemed to have more ice cream on their faces, flippers, and the table than in their dishes. *Come and sit with us,* she mouthed, *PLEASE!*

"Take a dish, and help yourself to two scoops of any flavor." Thelma pointed to some large tubs on a counter. "There are toppings on the tables: seaweed sprinkles, chocolate brine, krill mallows . . . When you're finished, make up a name for your ice cream creation and stick it in the ideas box. Be sure to put your name and address on the back, because once a month we choose one winner to receive a Frosters cap, just like mine— Oh my!" She covered her ears with her flippers. "What is that awful sound? It's definitely not the fire alarm, because I run the fire drill twice a week and it does not sound like that."

Jackson looked at Quigley. He had a pretty good idea what sort of alarm it was. The *intruder* sort!

"I'm gonna find out what's happening." Thelma shook her head, and a crab claw popped out of the side of her cap. "This is Thelma

MackFlipper contacting Control Center," she said, talking into the claw. "I'd like to know why an alarm is going off in the visitor center!"

Jackson nudged Quigley. *Look!* he mouthed. *Sunny's cap design!* Surely Quigley's cousin wasn't working for Frosters?

"Really?" Thelma frowned as she listened to whoever it was that she was communicating with via her cap. "There are two intruders in the factory, you say?"

Jackson gulped. But before he could suggest to Quigley that now would be the best time to make a run for it, the visitor center doors burst open and a group of angry-looking penguins thundered in. "There they are!" shouted the one at the front. "It's definitely them!"

Jackson groaned. It was the suspicious-looking penguin with the beak piercing who had been pushing the cart with the jewels inside. And behind her—Jackson tried not to meet his eye—was the pirate penguin from the laboratory; Fluffy, the gull, was perched on his flipper again.

"That's them, Mr. Blow Frost," the beak-stud penguin said again, pointing a flipper at them. "They had lab coats and goggles on before, but I'm sure that's them."

Every head in the room turned to stare at Jackson and Quigley. Lily looked worried. Thelma did, too. "Um, please, could some-one tell me what's going on here?" Thelma said, looking at Jackson and Quigley, then at the pirate penguin. "Mr. Blow Frost, sir?" she appealed to him. "These young penguins were on my tour, but they got lost looking for the bathroom and—"

Blow Frost, the pirate penguin, silenced her with a look, then strode across the room and poked Jackson sharply in the chest. "You've got something that belongs to me," he hissed. "Give it back!"

Jackson felt his cheeks burn; Blow Frost had to be talking about the ice cream tub he'd taken from the lab.

"I haven't g-g-got anything." Jackson gazed up into the small, mean eyes and all his secret-agent fibbing skills evaporated like ice cream on a stove top. *Maybe* he's *the evil hypnotist,* Jackson thought. *He's certainly turning my mind to mush.*

"Jackson! Quigley! It's time to go!" Lily darted across the room, moving between Jackson and Blow Frost. "If we don't go now, we'll be late for the paint-your-own-pottery party."

Blow Frost pushed past her. "I think you're industrial spies," he growled at Jackson. "You've come here to steal my ice cream secrets."

"I'm sure that's not true, Mr. Blow Frost," Thelma said. "They're just regular naughty little hatchlings. Didn't you say something about the penguins you're looking for wearing lab coats and goggles? Well, these youngsters are wearing regular clothes."

Blow Frost snorted, then shook his head and a crab claw popped out of his cap.

Jackson looked at Quigley. *Sunny's cap design, AGAIN!*

"This is Blow Frost to Control," he said into the crab claw. "Check all cap cams and security camera pictures."

Cap cams? Huh? Jackson glanced at Quigley. He shrugged.

"I want to know if any hatchlings have discarded lab coats and goggles somewhere in the factory." Blow Frost tapped his cap and the crab claw retracted.

Jackson shuffled uncomfortably. If the factory had security cameras, they were bound to have recorded him taking the ice cream. Not to mention him and Quigley stuffing the lab coats and goggles into their backpacks. Any minute now, Blow Frost would probably order a bag search, and then he'd find the ice cream. Jackson gulped. He glanced at the front doors, calculating how far they might get if they made a sudden run for it.

"Excuse me, sir." Lily stepped in front of

Blow Frost again. "It couldn't have been them. They were only gone a few minutes. They were with our group the rest of the time." She glanced at her wrist-flipper. "Oh, is that the time? Boy, we're late! Hey, guys," she called to her group of little hatchlings. "Come over here and help Jackson and Quigley out to the snowmobile. It's pottery time!"

The hatchlings squealed excitedly and shuffled over to surround Jackson and Quigley, their faces and flippers smeared with sticky ice cream. Blow Frost took a step backward, revulsion on his face. "Urgh, watch it!" he snapped. "Someone clean up these creatures!"

He shuddered. "I'm allergic to hatchlings," he muttered so quietly that only Jackson heard.

"Sure, sure," Thelma soothed. "Come on, kids, this way." She herded Lily and the hatchlings and Jackson and Quigley toward the doors. "I'll show you the bathrooms on the way out. Don't forget to stay on the blue footprints!"

"No! Stop! Not those two!" Blow Frost made a lunge for Jackson.

But Lily had pulled out her icePad. "Smile everyone!" she said, turning the camera on Blow Frost. "I'm filming this for my school project: *A Visitor's Guide to Rookeryville.* We've got to show everyone what an AMAZING place Frosters is for all the kids in Rookeryville to visit."

Blow Frost gritted his beak, but backed away.

Jackson felt Blow Frost's eyes on him all the way to the door. "Great trick with the icePad. Thanks so much, Lily," he whispered as they left the building. "We owe you."

"Well, you owe me an explanation," Lily said. "I'm guessing this is FBI business, right?"

Jackson took a deep breath. "My uncle Bryn has been hypnotized into becoming a bank robber and a jewel thief."

"No way!" Lily frowned. "That's terrible."

"Yeah," Quigley said. "And we think the Frosters ice cream he was eating may have had something to do with it."

Lily's eyes widened. "But I've been eating Frosters ice cream and I haven't been hypnotized."

"Yeah, but this stuff glows. Look." Jackson held open his bag.

"So that's what you took?" Lily sighed.

"Only as FBI evidence!" Jackson quickly closed the bag.

"I'm going to run some tests on it," Quigley

said. "It may have some synthetic enzymes that mess with the brain."

"So I'm guessing you don't want to come to the pottery party with me and my little cousins." Lily looked over at a taxi sled the sticky hatchlings were piling into. "I'm looking after them for my aunt. There was a robbery at the jewel store where she works last night, and she had to go in and check what's missing— Wait!" She blinked at Jackson. "Did your uncle rob my aunt's store?"

Jackson groaned. "Maybe. Look, I'm sorry, Lily. Uncle Bryn's not himself right now."

"Sure." Lily nodded. "But maybe you could come help me at the pottery party with my cousins to make up for it. It's not far. It's just next to Waddles' Department Store."

Jackson glanced at Quigley. *Waddles' Department Store!* If they went anywhere near there, Jackson's mom might spot them. He did not want to have to explain why they weren't at Quigley's house, like they were supposed to be. Jackson looked back at Lily.

"Pleeeease!" she said.

Jackson sighed. "Okay, I guess we owe you. We'll meet you there. But we need to go see someone on the way."

Quigley nodded. "My cousin Sunny!"

"I don't see him." Jackson wheeled his ice cycle past the different Rookeryville funfair rides on Windy Tail Pier—the Flying Clams, the bumper car seals, the Whirlpool roller coaster. He could never understand how Sunny had gotten the job designing and fixing the rides at the funfair. He was the most dangerous inventor penguin on the planet.

"Hey, you should see Sunny's latest plans for the new ride he's building," Quigley said. "It's called the Terror-Flipper Spin-a-Tron! You sit on this enormous spinning top thing that whizzes around really fast, then it spins you off, but you're on a bungee cord, so you just snap back onto it again. Neat, huh?"

Jackson tried to look enthusiastic. "Um—sounds awesome."

"Sunny's got a prototype in his yard. Look, I'll show you some pictures on my icePhone."

"Hey! Since when do you have a cell?" Jackson frowned. His mom would never let him have one.

"It's Sunny's old one. It was busted. He gave it to me last week. I only just fixed it. Look—there's the Spin-a-Tron."

Jackson glanced at the pictures on the screen. It looked even more terrifying than it sounded.

"You can come with me to Sunny's place to test it out sometime, if you want."

"Um—thanks." Jackson forced a smile. He'd rather go bowling with Blow Frost!

"Look," he said, changing the subject. "Up there!" He pointed to a distant figure in a red cap at the top of the waterwheel ride. "Isn't that Sunny?"

Quigley shielded his eyes from the sun. "Yeah, it is—SUNNY! SUNNY!" he bellowed. "Look, he's waving! Hey, I think he's telling us to climb up."

"Up there?" Jackson did a quick estimation. The waterwheel had to be at least a hundred and fifty flippers high.

But Quigley had already abandoned his ice

cycle and set off, scrambling under the safety barriers and dodging the spinning waterwheel cars as they passed by. "Come on!" he called, heading for the tiny metal cage ladder in the core of the ride. "Race you!"

Race you? Jackson looked up the cage ladder. *You've got to be kidding.* No way did he want to race up one of Sunny's scary rides on a rickety ladder with thin metal bars enclosing it.

"I can see a flame," Quigley called as they began to climb. "Sunny must be welding."

Either that, or he's set the wheel on fire and it's about to explode! Jackson gritted his beak. The higher they climbed, the more wobbly and unstable the structure felt. Jackson clung tighter to it as the wind whistled through his crest.

"Hey, cuz!" Jackson heard Sunny shout. "And yo! Cuz's friend!"

Despite the fact that Jackson and Quigley

had been best buddies since they were eggs, Sunny could never remember Jackson's name.

"Hi," Jackson said, crawling onto the platform at the top. *Is it my imagination or is this thing shaking?*

Sunny turned off his blowtorch. "I'm just fixing the supports. We don't want this old wheel to roll away, do we? Ha!"

Jackson tried to laugh, but it was hard on account of the wind doing its darnedest to blast him off the ride. He clung to the metal platform, trying not to think about what his mom would say if he got splattered across Windy Tail Pier.

"Hey—" Sunny peered at Jackson's feet. "Have you peed yourself?"

"What?" Jackson glanced down. A thick neon-yellow liquid was dribbling down his legs. "The ice cream!" He pulled off his backpack and extracted the melting tub. *Urgh*. He grimaced. The inside of his bag was swimming in it.

"Did you say *ice cream*?" Sunny dumped his tools and shuffled over. "I *love* ice cream. Cool color; let me try it."

Before Jackson could stop him, he'd dipped his flipper into the gooey ice cream and licked it.

"Sunny, no— Wait!" Jackson tried to pull the tub out of reach.

"Mmm," Sunny murmured, taking another dip-and-lick, then another, and another.

"Stop him!" Quigley shouted.

Jackson wrestled the tub away from Sunny. But Sunny lunged after it. There was only one way to stop him. Jackson hurled the tub over the side. *Oh, no! We needed that.* Then—*Please don't hit anyone on the head,* he thought, crossing his flippers and peering over the edge to check.

"Sunny?" Quigley prodded his cousin. "Are you okay?"

But Sunny didn't reply. He just stood there.

"Nooo!" Quigley groaned. "Now he looks a lot like your uncle."

"Like a zombie with brain freeze." Jackson waved his flipper in front of Sunny's face, but Sunny's gaze didn't change.

"So it *was* the ice cream that hypnotized your uncle Bryn." Quigley puffed out his cheeks. "But I still don't get it. How could it make him rob a bank? I mean, Sunny's not exactly doing much, is he." He patted his cousin's flipper and Sunny swayed slightly, but didn't move.

"Wait . . ." Jackson stared at Sunny, an idea beginning to form. "Maybe he just needs to be told what to do. Let me try something." Jackson stepped close to Sunny. "Sunny," he said, "stand on one leg."

Instantly, Sunny did as he was told.

Quigley's eyes widened.

"Sunny, touch your beak with your left flipper."

"He's doing it," Quigley shouted. "Look!"

"Sunny, pat the top of your cap twenty times. See, he just needs instruction," Jackson said. "Someone must have told Uncle Bryn to rob the banks."

"But we only saw your uncle and his friends in the jewelry store," Quigley said. "Who was telling him what to do?"

Jackson stared at Sunny some more, his eyes resting on the cap Sunny was patting. "The caps!" he said. "The Frosters workers were wearing caps. So was Uncle Bryn."

Quigley nodded slowly. "So you think he

was getting instructions from the speaker inside the cap. That makes sense. Sunny's cap is connected to his icePhone. If someone calls him, he hears their voice through a speaker inside it, so he doesn't have to stop working if he gets a call."

"Let me try something. Can I borrow your icePhone?"

Quigley handed it over.

"Is Sunny's number in here?"

Quigley leaned over and tapped the screen. Moments later, Sunny's hat began to bleep and the crab claw mouthpiece popped out.

Jackson took a deep breath. "Sunny," he whispered, speaking into the icePhone. "Say 'I'm a very silly penguin. Who makes extremely scary rides.'"

Quigley made a face at Jackson, but Sunny immediately repeated: "I'm a very silly penguin who makes extremely scary rides."

"That's it!" Quigley said. "The ice cream causes brain freeze, then someone takes over the penguin's mind by telling them what to do through the cap they're wearing."

"And I bet I know who!" Jackson spoke into the icePhone again. "Answer my questions, Sunny. Do you work for Blow Frost?"

"Yes, I make caps for Mr. Blow Frost!" Sunny said in a flat zombie voice.

"Why does Mr. Blow Frost want your caps?" Jackson asked.

Quigley crossed his flippers. "Please don't say you knew about the robberies."

"Mr. Blow Frost wants the caps to communicate with his workers in the factory," Sunny's zombie voice said.

"Phew." Quigley sighed with relief. "So he didn't know about the robberies."

"How do the caps work?" Jackson asked.

"There are cap cams on the front," Sunny said.

Cap cams? Jackson's eyes narrowed. Blow Frost had mentioned them.

"So Mr. Blow Frost can see what his workers see," Sunny explained. "There is a speaker inside the cap so he can tell them what to do."

Jackson nodded. "A genius idea," he said to Quigley. "I'm almost impressed. Blow Frost never has to leave his factory. He can get innocent ice cream lovers to carry out all his crimes, like an evil puppet master."

"Wonder how long the brain freeze lasts?" Quigley said, looking at his cousin.

"Well, he didn't eat much of it," Jackson said. "Not as much as Uncle Bryn. And speaking of Uncle Bryn, we need to go find him and get that cap off his head." Jackson glanced out across Rookeryville. "Wonder if we can spot the truck sled from up here?"

"I don't see it." Quigley peered over the edge. "But, hey, isn't that Hoff Rockface and his buddies down there? Looks like they're messing around, as usual."

"And no one will stop them because Hoff's dad owns the funfair." Jackson puffed out his cheeks. "I haven't forgotten we owe him payback. Wait . . ." He looked at Sunny, and then at the icePhone in his flipper. "I've just thought of another genius idea." He chuckled as he began dialing Sunny's number again. "Hoff Rockface, prepare to squirm!"

Climbing down off the giant waterwheel didn't take nearly as long as going up. Sunny went first, with an instruction from Jackson to wait for Quigley and him at the bottom.

"There's Hoff and his buddies," Jackson whispered to Quigley as they jumped down the last few rungs of the ladder. "Careful—don't let them see you."

Hoff Rockface and his friends were sitting on the Water Snails—a ride meant for tiny hatchlings. They were eating cotton candy and krill burgers and shouting at one another, scaring the two tiny hatchlings who were trying to enjoy their ride.

"They're so mean," Quigley muttered as the two tinies clambered off to get away from Hoff and his gang.

"Don't worry. I've got a plan." Jackson waited until the little ones were far enough away from the ride and then said into the icePhone, "Sunny: Go to the central control box. Don't let Hoff and his buddies see you. Use your tools to turn the Water Snails ride up really fast! Faster than that ride has ever gone before; as fast as the Spin-a-Tron!"

Sunny pulled a wrench out of his tool belt and trotted off.

Quigley's eyes widened. "Awesome idea!"

Jackson grinned. "Payback time."

Hoff Rockface and his buddies didn't notice Sunny heading to the control box. Or the gradual increase in speed. They just kept on goofing around, shouting and laughing and flicking cotton candy at one another. Then suddenly everything changed.

"Whoa!" Hoff lurched forward. "What the— OOF!" His cotton candy blasted back into his face. "Urgh!" he squealed, wiping his eyes and grabbing onto his snail's neck.

Jackson grinned at Quigley as Hoff and his friends whizzed past them.

"I didn't think a hatchling ride could go so fast," Quigley said.

"Yeah, and Hoff doesn't look like he's enjoying it much." Jackson smiled. "In fact, he looks pretty green. Whoa—watch it!" Jackson grabbed Quigley's flipper and tugged him out of the way of a spray of vomit that shot out of Hoff's beak as he zoomed past. "I guess snacks and fast rides don't mix too well."

"Uh-oh." Quigley glanced at the control box. "I think Sunny's brain freeze is wearing off."

In the control box Sunny was scratching his crest and shaking his head like he had water in his ears.

"Let me check," Jackson said, dialing Sunny's number on the icePhone again. "Sunny: Waggle your flippers in the air like you don't care," he said into it.

"Huh?" came Sunny's reply from the other end. "Who is this?"

Jackson handed the cell back to Quigley. "We'd better get out of here before he lets Hoff off that ride. He's going to be in one bad mood."

"Where to next?" Quigley said.

Jackson puffed out his cheeks. "I guess it's the pottery place. We made a promise to Lily. But it'll have to be quick."

"Yeah, because your uncle Bryn could be robbing another store right this minute!"

"Worse than that." Jackson shuddered. "Mom might spot us!"

They pulled up behind a dumpster in a parking lot close to the paint-your-own-pottery place—and right next to Waddles' Department Store.

Jackson peeked out. "Okay, we'll need to make a run for it. As long as Mom's not looking out one of the windows, we should be okay, and—"

"Um—Jackson," Quigley interrupted. "Check out that truck sled over there."

Jackson looked where Quigley was pointing. And then he saw it. He gripped the handlebars of his ice cycle, his beak twitching, his flippers tingling. "It's here!" he gasped. "The ice cream truck sled."

Jackson and Quigley watched the back doors of the ice cream truck sled clank open and three penguins wearing caps jump out.

Jackson's feathers stood on end. "It's Uncle Bryn!" he spluttered—or would have, if his throat hadn't felt like it had six starfish stuck in it.

"It looks like they're eating something," Quigley said, squinting to see better.

"Ice cream!" Jackson hissed. "Brain-freezing ice cream. That must mean they're about to do another robbery. We've got to stop them."

"Maybe we should call the FBI," Quigley suggested.

"No way!" Jackson puffed out his cheeks. "They'll just arrest them . . . If only we could get the caps off their heads— Oh no—they're on the move."

They watched the three penguins throw their empty ice cream tubs into a trash can and shuffle across the parking lot.

Jackson gasped. "I don't believe it! They're heading for"—he gulped for air—"Waddles'! Uncle Bryn's about to rob Mom's work!"

This was a gold-plated, force-ten, max-power ultimate disaster! Jackson's mom was an award-winning store detective. If Uncle Bryn tried to steal anything from under her beak, Jackson knew she'd be on to him in a flash.

His mom would hate having to arrest Uncle Bryn. But if she didn't, she would probably lose her job. Jackson sighed.

It was already too late to try to stop them. Uncle Bryn and his two colleagues had disappeared through the back door of Waddles'.

"What are we going to do?" Jackson ran his flipper through his crest. *Think, 00Zero!* he told himself. *There has to be some way to fix this.*

"Hey—that's interesting," Quigley said. He was peering through his bin-ice-ulars at the truck sled. "An antenna's just popped up on the sled's roof."

"So?" Jackson tried to look interested. But he knew it wasn't working.

"It's a transmitter aerial," Quigley explained. "Which means the ice cream truck could be the control hub for the caps."

"Say that again," Jackson said, "in normal-penguin language."

"Someone in the ice cream truck is probably controlling your uncle," Quigley said. "It makes sense. It's much easier to transmit messages if you're close by. There's less chance of interference. And that transmitter aerial suggests that the person controlling your uncle Bryn is probably inside the truck!"

"Blow Frost?"

"Or one of his workers."

Jackson felt his heart begin to beat faster. *Maybe we aren't too late to stop Uncle Bryn.* "Quigley! You're a genius!" He slapped his buddy on the back. "All we need to do is get inside the truck and WE can control Uncle Bryn. We can stop him before he robs Mom's store." He glanced up at the brown building. "It's got to have at least six floors. It might take him a while to find the target, whatever that is."

"Fancy purses?" Quigley suggested. "Mom always likes looking at them. But she says they're way too pricey to buy."

"Maybe. But whatever they're after, we have to stop them. Come on, quick! Let's do this!"

"Just one thing . . . How are we going to get whoever is in there out of it?" Quigley asked as he followed Jackson across the parking lot.

"Like this!" Jackson banged his flipper on the side of the truck sled. "Hello, hello! Open up! We—um—want to buy an ice cream!"

Quigley glanced through the windshield, but no one was in the front seats. "They must be in the back of the truck," he whispered, pulling out his bin-ice-ulars again. He flipped a switch on the side, then peered through the dark glass covering the side windows. "There's definitely two penguins in there," he whispered. "The infrared mode on my bin-ice-ulars is picking up their body heat."

Jackson felt a slight wobble in his tummy; taking on two baddies controlling a robbery was a big deal. *But I've got to do this for Uncle Bryn,* he reminded himself. He stared at the truck sled again. "There has to be some way to get them out."

"Well, I do have one idea." Quigley rummaged through his backpack. "It's my latest and greatest secret-agent field weapon. Ta-da!"

"Blowing bubbles?" Jackson groaned. "Neat, but I don't think blowing bubbles at the windows is going to make them leave."

"These are no ordinary bubbles." Quigley popped off the lid and took out the wand. "Watch . . ." As he blew, a stream of green bubbles drifted over to Jackson.

"I love bubbles as much as the next penguin," Jackson began, wafting them away with his flipper. "But we don't have time for—URGH!" Jackson suddenly covered his beak and made a yuck face. "Smells worse than Hoff Rockface's farts! What is that?"

"Barf bubbles!" Quigley said. "Guaranteed to clear a room in ten seconds. All we need to do is get them to open a window so I can blow some in, then they'll be out of that ice cream truck sled before we can say *one scoop or two*!"

"Nice one, Agent Q, but if they won't be able to stand the smell in there, how will we?"

"Because we'll be wearing these." Quigley passed Jackson a clothespin. "Just stick one over your beak. You won't smell a thing."

"But we still need to get them to open up. Maybe we could pick the door lock or something. Have you got a crest pin?"

Quigley shook his head. "I don't—but Lily might. Look!"

Across the parking lot, Lily and the young penguins were leaving the pottery place. She waved when she saw them heading over.

"Hey, Jackson. Hey, Quigley," Lily said. "Did you come to do some pottery? We just finished. But you can come to the aquarium with us if you like." *PLEASE,* she mouthed, glancing at the giggling hatchlings, who were now covered in paint as well as sticky ice cream. "My dad's giving us a tour. It'll be really neat and—"

"I'm sorry, Lily, we can't." Jackson glanced

at his wrist-flipper. They were running out of time. "Have you got a crest pin?"

She frowned. "Nope. Why?"

"We have to break into that truck sled." Jackson pointed across the lot. "There are two penguins inside who are controlling my uncle. He's in Waddles' Department Store, about to rob it—and they're giving him instructions!"

Lily's eyes widened. "Really?"

Quigley nodded. "But if we can open a door or a window of the truck sled, I've got these awesome bubbles to blow inside that really stink."

"They stink so bad, the penguins will jump out," Jackson said. "Then we can get in and tell my uncle to quit robbing. But we haven't got much time!"

Lily eyed the truck sled for a moment. Then she glanced back at the boys. "I haven't got a crest pin. But I've got another idea." She beckoned the hatchlings closer. "Listen up, guys. My friends need your help."

"We do?" Jackson looked at Quigley.

"Pay attention, everyone!" Lily told the hatchlings. "This is really important. And we need to work quickly."

"So does everyone know what we're doing?" Lily asked the hatchlings. They were gathered beside the truck sled now. "We're going to sing really loudly!" She turned to Jackson and Quigley and whispered, "Like the worst, most annoying street performers you've ever heard. Then the baddie penguins inside will get so fed up with us, they'll open their window and tell us to go away."

Jackson crossed his flippers. *Please let this work.*

Lily turned back to the little penguins.

"Okay, here we go. One, two, three: *She'll be coming 'round the iceberg, when she comes! She'll be coming 'round the iceberg when she comes! Singing aye aye flippy . . .*"

As Lily launched into the song, the hatchlings, still giggling and nudging one another, began joining in. Quigley moved closer to the truck sled windows, his bubble wand at the ready.

"*She'll be wearing shrimp pajamas when she comes. She'll be wearing shrimp pajamas when she comes,*" sang Lily and the hatchlings.

Come on, come on, Jackson stared at the windows of the truck sled, willing them to open.

"*She'll be swimming with a seahorse when she comes . . . ,*" sang Lily and the hatchlings. Then suddenly the truck sled window shot open and a flipper-full of coins were thrown out. "Now go away!" a voice shouted from inside. "And don't come back!"

It was just the chance Quigley needed. He jumped forward and blew in the bubbles just as the window closed.

Then—

"Argh!"

"Urgh!"

The truck sled doors crashed open and two chunky penguins in Frosters caps fell out, coughing and moaning.

Jackson, his clothespin on his beak, barged past them and dived inside, closely followed by Quigley. "Lock the doors!" he shouted.

The Frosters penguins began hammering on the doors. "Get out of our truck!" one yelled.

But Jackson didn't notice. He was gazing at a wall of screens inside the truck sled. On all the monitors was the same picture—a close-up of a giant metal safe, its door open and piles of cash being emptied into a sack.

"It's Uncle Bryn!" Jackson gasped, the horrible wobbly feeling returning to his tummy. "I'd recognize those flippers anywhere. We're too late. He's robbing Waddles' safe."

"There's still time," Quigley said. "Look, that's the microphone." He twisted it toward Jackson. "Speak into it."

Jackson took a deep breath. "This is, um—Control Hub to Bryn Rockflopper. Stop robbing that safe immediately!"

Instantly the flippers on the screen froze.

"It's working," Quigley whispered.

"Put all the money back in the safe!" Jackson said, holding his breath and staring at the screen.

"He's doing it!" Quigley said. "Look! His buddies are helping, too."

More loud thumps on the truck sled doors made him and Jackson jump. The penguins outside were yelling and cursing now. They began to rock the truck sled.

Jackson braced himself against the control desk, then leaned into the microphone again. "When you have put the money back inside the safe," he told his uncle, "close the safe door and return to the truck sled. Hurry!" he added as the truck sled bounced wildly again.

"Jackson!" Quigley shouted. "Your backpack's bleeping."

"What? No, not the FBI radio!" Jackson grabbed the bag. He had a bad feeling about this.

Calling all agents,
calling all agents.
A robbery is underway at Waddles' Department Store. Rogue agent Bryn Rockflopper has been spotted on security cameras.
All agents respond!

"Disaster!" Jackson gasped. "If the FBI comes now, they're going to think *we're* part of the robbery. No way will they believe that we're trying to stop it."

“That means Blow Frost will get away with everything!” Quigley said. “What are we going to do?”

Jackson ran his flipper through his crest. He stood up from the control panel and gritted his beak. “The only thing we can do—escape!”

"You can drive, right?" Quigley said, as he and Jackson peered over at the front seats of the truck sled.

"Not exactly." Jackson scratched his crest. "But, hey, how hard can it be? Grown-ups do it all the time, and I haven't played one adult at *Flipper Cart Racing* on the Icebox who can beat me. I never crash— Whoa!" he yelled as the truck sled rocked sideways again. "Sheesh! Those penguins must be super mad."

"Here comes your uncle!" Quigley said, pointing out the window. He leaned over to unlock the doors. But before Uncle Bryn reached them, the two baddie penguins barged in. "Hey—no, get off me!" Quigley yelled as the one with a curly crest grabbed his flippers.

The second penguin, smaller but stockier and smelling of krill chili, dived for Jackson. "Gotcha!" he growled.

Jackson managed to slip out of his flippers and grab the microphone again. "Agent Rockflopper!" he shouted into it. "Come to the truck sled immediately! You and your colleagues need to flipper-cuff the two rotten Frosters penguins attacking me and my friend! And whatever they say, DO NOT listen to any more instructions from any penguin wearing a Frosters cap— Ahhh! Get off!"

"I'll teach you to try and steal our truck sled," the stinky penguin muttered.

Jackson felt a bubble of anger balloon in

his belly. *Got to use some moves from the* Secret Agent's Guide to Unarmed Flipper-to-Flipper Combat, Jackson told himself. *Time to unleash the "peck, flick, and run" move.*

The peck part worked. Jackson pulled off his clothespin and beak-biffed the baddie in the belly. The flick bit was pretty awesome, too. Jackson flipper-flicked him in the eye. But the run part was an epic fail on account of the bad-breathed penguin being so angry by then that he clamped his flippers around Jackson and squeezed.

Jackson yelped as the breath shot out of his lungs. "I'm not a tube of beak paste!" he wanted to shout, but there was no air left in his chest to speak. But then—

"Unhand that hatchling!" Bryn and his two colleagues dived into the back of the truck sled and began wrestling with the two Frosters baddies.

Jackson felt a wave of relief wash over him. This was the Uncle Bryn he knew—fighting bad guys, making everything better.

"Wow, this is some party!" Lily said, peeking in through the door. "I think we're going to go now. Hey, what's that noise?" She glanced behind her. "Um—Jackson, there are some serious-looking sleds heading your way."

Jackson dodged around the wrestling grown-ups and poked his head through the truck sled door. Six shiny black sleds were speeding into the parking lot. "The FBI!

We've got to go! Thanks so much for your help, Lily. I promise we'll make it up to you." Jackson ducked back inside and slipped into the front seat of the truck sled. He turned the ignition key and the engine chugged to life.

"Yeah, thanks, Lily. You guys were awesome," Quigley said, pulling the door of the truck sled closed. He slipped past the grown-ups, who were still shouting and wrestling and bouncing around in the back of the truck.

"Just give me a second," Jackson said as Quigley slid into the seat next to him. He was gazing at the driver's panel, a wave of panic sweeping through his feathers. If only he had an Icebox controller.

"Hey, isn't that your mom out there?" Quigley said.

Jackson glanced through the windshield and felt his feathers freeze. There, head down, feet flapping, flipper-cuffs swinging from her belt, was Jackson's mom, coming straight for them. Jackson gulped. *Please don't spot me, please don't spot me.* He shimmied down into the footwell of the driver's seat, scrunching himself as low as he could go to avoid her glare.

"She looks mad!" Quigley said. "But don't worry, I've got a plan to get us out of here. I just iglooogled 'How to operate dangerous criminal ice cream truck sleds' and found a video on my icePad. See?" He turned the screen around to show Jackson, then flipped it back. "Just hit the right-hand pedal and put the gearshift into drive—yep, exactly like that— Whoa!"

The truck sled lurched forward, nearly knocking Jackson's mom over. Jackson spun the wheel hard to the left, and they just had time to see her face go Great White as she locked eyes with Jackson before they whizzed past her and out of the parking lot.

"Maybe she didn't see you," Quigley said.

"She saw me!" Jackson gasped, spinning the wheel to the right and screeching around the corner. "Didn't you see her face? Sheesh!" He shuddered. "She's gonna go off the Shark Scale when she catches up with me. What's happening back there?" he added. "It's awfully quiet."

Quigley twisted around and leaned into the back to check. "Good news," he said, sliding back into place a moment later. "Your uncle's got them cuffed and strapped in, and he even put clothespins on their beaks to keep them quiet."

"Awesome," Jackson muttered.

"Yeah, but I think we're being followed," Quigley added, pointing to the side mirror. "Looks like the FBI is on our tail, and hey—is that your mom?"

Jackson glanced in his mirror and felt his belly turn to liquid. "Festering fin feathers!" he spluttered. "She's riding my bike!" He hit the accelerator pedal and the truck sled shot forward.

"Err, where exactly are we going?" Quigley asked, holding on to the door handle because the truck sled was whizzing along like a Formula 1 racer.

Jackson shrugged. He hadn't quite worked out that bit of the escape plan yet. Driving in a straight line seemed to be enough of a battle right now. "Sorry!" he shouted as several old-age penguins in a pedestri-penguin crosswalk had to jump back onto the sidewalk to avoid being mowed down.

"I don't want to worry you," Quigley said. "But I think two more FBI sleds have joined the posse." Quigley peered in his mirror again. "And I have no idea how your mom is keeping up."

"Bionic legs," Jackson muttered. He'd always suspected his mom was part cyborg.

As they whizzed around the next corner, a loud buzzing came from the dashboard and a crackly voice sounded:

"This is Frosters Control Room to Truck Sled X. Can you hear me? We seem to have lost contact; please confirm your position."

Jackson's eyes narrowed. "Frosters!" he breathed. "Of course! Frosters Factory! That's where we're going!"

"We are?" Quigley raised his eyebrows.

"Yep." Jackson gripped the steering wheel more tightly. "And we're taking the FBI with us. We're going to lead them straight to Blow Frost. Once we're inside the factory, we'll be able to show them the secret laboratory and the weird brain-freezing ice cream and prove Uncle Bryn is innocent!" Jackson pointed to a walkie-talkie on the dash. "Can you hold that thing up toward me?" he said. "Yeah, a bit closer." He took a deep breath: "THIS IS

TRUCK SLED X," Jackson shouted into the walkie-talkie. "We're on our way back to base and we have an urgent delivery for Mr. Blow Frost. Please have him standing by for our arrival!"

"Wow!" Quigley flipped off the walkie-talkie. "Neat plan—" Then, "Uh-oh," he added, glancing out of Jackson's window. "We've got company!"

Jackson followed his stare and looked straight into the face of an FBI penguin. The FBI sled he was riding in had pulled up level with them.

"PULL OVER!" the FBI penguin shouted through a megaphone. "Or we will force you off the road."

Jackson put his foot down on the accelerator and the ice cream truck sled zoomed forward, nearly smacking into the back of a dumpster truck ahead of them. "Ahhh!" Jackson veered onto the other side of the road to overtake it, narrowly missing a bus coming the other way.

"Whoa!" Quigley breathed. "Awesome driving!"

"Thanks. We're nearly at the docks now— Wait—what's that sign saying?" Jackson hit the brakes and slowed down. A stoplight was showing up ahead, and traffic had begun to line up behind it.

"Roadwork!" Quigley groaned. He glanced in his mirror. "And here comes the FBI again."

"But if we stop now, they'll arrest us and

Blow Frost will get away with it all. There's got to be another way." Jackson took his foot off the accelerator, looking desperately for a place to turn off the highway.

"Hold on one minute—" Quigley was peering at the dashboard. "If we can't go around them," he muttered, "maybe we can go over them! Don't you remember what my dad said about the gear system he'd installed in a fleet of ice cream truck sleds? The hopper gear."

"But we don't even know if it was for Frosters," Jackson said.

"There!" Quigley pointed to a small red button at the bottom of the dash. "If I was putting a hopper gear into a truck sled, I'd put the control in exactly that place. It's gotta be the right button."

"What if you're wrong?" Jackson glanced in his mirror. The FBI sleds were right behind them now. And so was his mom.

"What's the worst that could happen?" Quigley grinned.

Jackson took a deep breath and wished for the best. "I hope your dad doesn't put self-destruct buttons on *his* inventions." He gritted his beak. "Okay. Let's do this!"

Then he hit the button.

Quigley shut his eyes. Jackson held his breath. And the grown-ups in the back (minus the still-zombified Uncle Bryn and his two colleagues) let out a loud but muffled *OMG* as the truck sled shot skyward, up and over the traffic, bunny-hop style.

Jackson gripped the steering wheel, his eyes popping. The hopper gear *had* worked! They were now soaring over the line of traffic. Jackson almost felt like waving to the startled penguins below. Almost—

"My dad's a genius, right?" Quigley beamed

out the window. "We must be forty flippers high." Then suddenly he stopped smiling. He glanced at Jackson. "Uhh—I wonder how this thing lands?"

Jackson had no time to reply because the truck sled had stopped soaring and was now dropping out of the air—dead-duck style.

KA-THWUMP!

Jackson felt his bones rattle as the truck sled smacked back down onto the road, just missing a digger-flipper ripping up the pavement.

Jackson blinked. He caught his breath and gave himself a thorough shake. *Nope, nothing broken.* Then he pressed the accelerator pedal. No way was it going to work after that crash— "Huh? We're still moving," he gasped. Admittedly, they weren't going quite as fast as before. In fact, they were crawling now, half-squished-snail style.

"There's Frosters over there," Quigley said as they crawled down Drift Wood Docks.

"We'll need to keep our faces down," Jackson said, "so the security guards don't see us."

But as the truck limped toward the gate, the security penguin didn't even look up from his clipboard. He just waved the truck sled through.

"This is it," Jackson said, driving into the loading dock. "Hope the FBI doesn't take too long to catch up with us."

Quigley checked the mirrors. "Nope, they're

right behind us—but they've been stopped at the gate by security. I don't see your mom, though. I guess she ran out of puff."

Phew! Jackson was WAY more terrified of seeing his mom than meeting Blow Frost! Then he spotted Blow Frost standing menacingly in the loading dock with his gull on his flipper, his nasty little eyes glaring out at them, surrounded by a gang of large muscle-penguins, and suddenly Jackson wasn't so sure. "Okay, here goes nothing." He pulled up next to Blow Frost and reached for his door handle. "Everyone out!" he shouted, and he and Quigley, Uncle Bryn and his colleagues, and the two flipper-cuffed bad penguins all tumbled out of the truck sled onto the loading dock.

"Sorry, boss!" the stinky, bad penguin tried to mumble through his clothespinned beak.

But Blow Frost silenced him with a stare. He gazed from one end of the line of passengers to the other, then back again. Then his eyes shrank to pinpricks and a rumbling came from his throat. "YOU!" he blasted at Jackson. "I knew you were trouble!"

Jackson gulped. His legs had gone slightly spaghetti under the death-ray gaze of Blow Frost. But then he reminded himself of who he was. *You're a secret agent! You can do this!* And he stepped forward, his head held high. "I'm arresting you on behalf of the FBI for using mind-altering ice cream to turn innocent penguins into zombie robbers! We've got all the evidence we need." He pointed at Uncle Bryn and his two buddies, who were all standing, staring into space, still in a trance.

"Ha!" Blow Frost cackled. "Seize them!" And his group of muscle-penguins leaped forward and pinned Jackson and Quigley by the flippers.

"So you worked it all out, did you?" Blow Frost sneered at Jackson and Quigley. "Well, aren't you clever. But soon I'll have enough cash from my little robberies to build another twenty ice cream factories full of brain-freezing, mind-altering ice cream, and then every penguin in Rookeryville will be turned into my zombie-penguin slave. Mwha-ha-ha-ha! Take them to the deep freeze!" he added to his muscle-penguins.

"I don't think so," Jackson said. "Look over there."

Blow Frost spun around to see a line of sleek FBI sleds speeding toward them. But the smile didn't leave his face.

"FREEZE!" FBI agents poured out of the sleds, ice lasers pointing, flipper-cuffs dangling, as they swarmed around the group.

Jackson felt a ripple of joy in his belly. At last, they'd arrest the real bad guys. But then—

"No wait! Don't flipper-cuff Uncle Bryn!" Jackson dodged free from the muscle-penguin who was holding him and darted over to where Senior Agent Frost-Flipper was reading Uncle Bryn and his colleagues their rights.

"We're arresting you for grand theft," Agent Frost-Flipper told Uncle Bryn and his friends. "And for violation of the FBI code of conduct, not to mention being all-around bad eggs!"

"Stop! You've got it all wrong!" Jackson tried to interrupt.

But Blow Frost pushed past him. "Oh, thank

you so much, officer." He shot a slimy, slippery sort of a smile at Senior Agent Frost-Flipper and stroked his gull. "Fluffy!" he told the bird. "Say thank you to this lovely, kind officer." The gull let out a squawk and Blow Frost beamed even more. "Those terrible penguins stole my ice cream truck sled." He pointed to Uncle Bryn and his friends. "Then they kidnapped my workers." He gestured to the flipper-cuffed bad penguins. And now they've come back here to try to rob me at my own factory!"

"That's not true," Jackson yelled at Blow Frost. "It was all YOU!"

Blow Frost's smile vanished.

"Jackson's right!" Quigley shouted. "It wasn't his uncle who did it. Well, it was, because he *did* technically carry out the robberies, but you see it wasn't really—"

"Enough!" Senior Agent Frost-Flipper silenced them. "I told you kids to stay out of

FBI business. I will be talking to your moms." She turned back to her agents. "Take rogue agent Rockflopper here and agents Feather-Freckle and Beak-Piddle straight to jail!"

And suddenly Uncle Bryn and his two colleagues were being bundled into the back of an FBI sled.

"No! Stop! You can't do this!" Jackson wailed. "Please, you have to listen to me!"

But Agent Frost-Flipper had turned her back on him. "I'm so sorry, Mr. Blow Frost," she said. "We'll be leaving now."

"No!" Jackson bellowed.

"Not another word!" Senior Agent Frost-Flipper snapped, and she turned to go.

Jackson felt a wild pulsing in his belly. He was a volcano on the verge of exploding. The lava was churning in his belly. Around and around. Up and down, thrashing his insides. Then he erupted.

"CODE RED!" he yelled to Quigley, and suddenly he was running.

"Lock the doors!" Jackson yelled as he and Quigley dived into the ice cream truck sled. "We've got to stop the FBI from leaving!"

Please work, please work, Jackson begged as he turned the ignition key and the engine spluttered to life. He put his foot down, and the battered vehicle jerked slowly forward.

"So—um, what's the plan?" Quigley said, sliding into the seat next to him.

"We're going to block the gate!" Jackson said. "Then go back and make them listen!"

"Great, but that security penguin looks pretty mad. He's shaking his clipboard at you."

"How do I put this into reverse?" Jackson demanded as he maneuvered the truck sled in front of the gate.

"Press that pedal, and I'll change the gear."

Jackson reversed into position, then turned off the engine. "Okay, I spotted a mini fridge in the back. That must be where they store the mind-altering ice cream. Grab some tubs and let's go do this!"

Moments later they burst out of the back of the truck sled. Flippers full of ice cream, heads down, they ran, dodging FBI agents, security guards, and baddie muscle-penguins. Feet flapping, they thundered over to Senior Agent Frost-Flipper, who was staring at them, her eyes as wide as dinner plates. "What on earth—" she began as Jackson flung a tub of ice cream into her flippers and spilled out the whole story in one long jumbled spew of information.

"—and just look at that ice cream if you still don't believe me." He panted. "It glows!" Jackson ripped off the lid of the tub in her flippers, and the neon ice cream gleamed in the sunlight.

"I can explain!" Blow Frost stalked over, the gull on his flipper squawking wildly. "That's experimental ice cream that those horrible little hatchlings must have stolen from my laboratory. I guess 'thieving flippers' must run in that penguin's family." He glared at Jackson.

But Senior Agent Frost-Flipper didn't answer. She was peering at the ice cream. "Weird!" She looked at Blow Frost. "I've never seen ice cream like this before."

"That's because it's new! Trust me, everyone's going to be eating it soon." Blow Frost tried to swipe the tub out of her flippers, but she stepped away from him.

"And you say your uncle was eating this before he started robbing banks and jewelry stores?" she asked Jackson.

He nodded.

"Coincidence!" Blow Frost exploded. "Don't tell me you believe that fibbing hatchling. Who ever heard of a mind-altering ice cream? Ridiculous! Now give it back!"

But Senior Agent Frost-Flipper stepped farther back, holding the tub out of his reach.

Jackson felt a tiny pimple of hope. The tide was turning; he could feel it in his feathers. "If there's nothing wrong with the ice cream," he said, waggling a tub under Blow Frost's beak, "then YOU eat it!"

"Me?" Blow Frost's face turned puce. "Eat it now?" He glanced at Senior Agent Frost-Flipper, a slight sweaty sheen appearing on his feathers. "You don't seriously believe these wild accusations?"

She shrugged. "It wouldn't hurt for you to prove them wrong."

"Fine!" Blow Frost hissed. He reached down and pretended to dip his flipper into the tub Jackson held out. "Mmm, so yummy," he said, licking his flipper. "Now can you all clear out of my factory and let me get back to making ice cream?"

"You didn't taste it!" Jackson said. "You did exactly what every kid does when their mom asks them to try stuff they know they'll hate."

"Yeah, like that slice of jellied eel brain pie Mom gave me last week." Quigley shuddered. "She told me I only had to have one tiny taste, so I PRETENDED to try it, but I didn't really."

"Yep, classic fake tasting!" Jackson said.

Blow Frost's face darkened. "Don't you dare accuse me—"

"But I can help you taste it properly," Jackson interrupted. "Poop Protector Hat!" he muttered to Quigley. But his buddy was already onto it, rummaging in his backpack.

"Huh?" Blow Frost stared at them, his beak open in surprise. It was just the opening Jackson needed. Quick as lightning, he grabbed one of the spoons on the hat from Quigley's bag, dipped it in the ice cream, and shoved it into Blow Frost's mouth.

"How dare you!" spluttered Blow Frost, spitting out the ice cream, but Jackson shoved in another spoonful. And another. "Stop!" Blow Frost batted him away. But then he suddenly stopped batting and spluttering and shouting and—

Froze.

"Mr. Blow Frost?" Senior Agent Frost-Flipper said. "Sir? Are you okay? You look a bit—"

"Zombified?" Jackson suggested.

"Brain-frozen?" Quigley added.

"Mind-altered?" Jackson said with a smile.

Senior Agent Frost-Flipper gave them a stern look. "Mr. Blow Frost?" She prodded him, but the evil penguin just stood there, staring into the distance.

"Don't worry. It will wear off soon," Jackson explained. "So we'd better hurry." He turned to face Blow Frost. "Mr. Blow Frost, tell us the truth."

"The truth," Blow Frost repeated in a zombie voice.

"Do you make mind-altering ice cream?"

"Yes," Blow Frost said.

"Did you take over my uncle's favorite snack shack for the day so you could feed him mind-altering ice cream that turned him into a bank-robbing zombie?"

"Yes," Blow Frost said.

"Are all the money and jewels that he stole on your behalf stashed somewhere in the factory?"

"Yes. They are in the big cupboard at the back of my office."

Senior Agent Frost-Flipper gasped.

Jackson nodded. "It was a clever plan. There's a speaker inside every Frosters cap," he explained, "so Blow Frost was able to give commands to Uncle Bryn and his colleagues."

"Plus there's a camera in the front, so he could see what they were doing," Quigley pointed out. "It's actually my cousin Sunny's design."

"But he's NOT involved!" Jackson added quickly. "He had no clue what the caps were to be used for."

Senior Agent Frost-Flipper nodded. "So

you boys were"—she coughed and cleared her throat—"right all along."

Jackson nodded. "Now will you let my uncle Bryn go?"

"Of course!" Senior Agent Frost-Flipper said. "And I should probably give you boys a medal."

"Or maybe you could just let us join the FBI," Jackson suggested.

But before Senior Agent Frost-Flipper could reply—

"Absolutely not!" shouted a familiar voice.

Her face shrimp-pink, her feathers flat with sweat, and her temper already maxing out on the Shark Scale of Crossness, Jackson's mom stomped over to the group. "Would someone please tell me what is going on here?"

Jackson felt his feathers shrivel under her gaze. "I-I-I can explain," he spluttered, trying to meet her eye. But he wasn't altogether sure he wanted to. Luckily, he didn't have to, because at just that moment there was a shout from behind them.

"Hello? Hello?"

Jackson spun around. "Uncle Bryn!"

He was lumbering toward them, rubbing his crest and yawning.

"Hey, Jackson, good to see you! Guess what?" he said. "I just woke up in the back of that sled. Weird, eh?" He suddenly noticed the other FBI agents. "Oh, hi, guys—err, good to see you, too. I just had the strangest dream." He shook his head and blinked. "There was this weird glowing ice cream and I was robbing banks and—" He spotted his boss. "Senior Agent Frost-Flipper!" he squeaked. "And Marina?" He blinked at Jackson's mom. "Um—what are you all doing here?" He looked around, suddenly noticing the factory, all the worker penguins, and Blow Frost still in a trance. "Um—where ARE we exactly?"

"It's a long story," Jackson said, glancing at his mom. "But me and Quigley will fill you in. It may take some time. Let's walk." *As far away from here as possible!*

"It could be worse," Quigley said as he handed a tub of ice cream to a small hatchling. "We could have been put back on deck-cleaning duty."

Jackson grimaced. "I think I'd prefer that. This costume is so hot." He scratched inside his fluffy ice cream cone hood and wished for the hundredth time that he'd never agreed to this plan.

It was a few days after the whole ice cream adventure, and Jackson's mom had arranged for them to help out at Brain Freezers for the day as punishment for sticking their beaks into FBI business again. Jackson had hoped he'd be working behind the counter making amazing ice cream sundaes. But instead, he and Quigley were out in the park, selling tubs of ice cream from Victor's mobile cart. Unfortunately, they were also dressed as giant ice cream cones. After all the bad publicity about Frosters' mind-altering frozen treats, Victor had been worried people might not want to eat ice cream anymore. But Jackson and Quigley had been running off their flippers.

Jackson scratched his itchy neck again. "You'd think Mom would be pleased we'd saved Uncle Bryn from a life of crime."

Quigley nodded. "Yeah, but I'm not sure she approved of the other stuff: driving without a license, endangering the lives of pedestri-penguins, and very nearly getting ourselves imprisoned in the deep freeze at Frosters Factory!"

Jackson sighed. "I guess not."

Life in Rookeryville had snapped back to normal pretty quickly after Blow Frost's arrest. Uncle Bryn and his two colleagues had taken a few days' vacation at the FBI rest center for a complete ice cream detox. All the stolen jewels and money had been found in the factory and safely returned to the rightful owners. And Frosters Factory had been put up for sale.

"I wish we could buy it," Quigley said. "Imagine owning your own ice cream factory!"

Jackson shuddered. "Yeah, imagine! I think I'm kind of over ice cream— Hey, look, there's Lily and the hatchlings. Lily! Over here!"

"Hi, Jackson. Hi, Quigley." Lily smiled. "It was kind of you to call; the hatchlings are so excited to get ice cream."

"No problem," Jackson said, flipping open the cart lid so the little penguins could see inside. "It's the least we could do after all your help." He pulled his backpack out from under the cart and rummaged inside for his wallet.

"Did your mom stop your allowance, too?" Quigley whispered, digging some coins out of his own bag.

Jackson nodded. "I'm using savings." He smiled at the hatchlings. "Okay, help yourselves to any tub you want. Me and Quigley are paying."

As the little ones reached for their ice creams, Jackson heard a horrible laugh.

"Check out the ice cream loser patrol!"

Jackson groaned. *Hoff Rockface!*

"Hey, Jackson. Love your costume," Hoff said. "This will make an awesome picture for my *Visitor's Guide to Rookeryville.* Smile for the camera!"

Jackson shut his eyes and wished the sidewalk could swallow him up sucking-squid style. Maybe scooping poop wasn't so bad after all.

"Selfie!" Hoff said, turning the camera

around so he was in the shot, too. "Come on, Jackson, smile!"

Jackson gritted his beak. Now everyone at school would see him in his ice cream costume.

"I want a free ice cream, too!" Hoff said, leaning into the cart.

"Huh?" Jackson glared at him. "No way!"

"You gave them free ice cream." Hoff scowled at the hatchlings. "I saw."

"No, we didn't. Me and Quigley are paying for them."

"It's true," Lily said. "They are using their own money."

"Don't believe you." Hoff's eyes narrowed. "If you don't give me an ice cream, I'll tell Victor you gave your buddies freebies."

Jackson felt a bubble of anger growing in his belly. He was about to tell Hoff to take a long hike off a tall iceberg when Hoff reached in and grabbed a tub from the back.

"Hey!" Jackson shouted. "Give that back!"

But Hoff had already ripped off the lid. He smirked at Jackson, then dipped his flipper into the ice cream.

Jackson gasped. He'd suddenly noticed the weird color of the ice cream Hoff was eating—the weird NEON color!

"Uh-oh!" Quigley muttered, shooting a worried glance at Jackson.

"Um, Hoff, I don't think you should eat that," Jackson said. "No, seriously, stop eating it NOW!"

But Hoff kept on slurping it out of the tub.

Jackson looked at Quigley. "Is that what I think it is?" he muttered.

"I think so," Quigley whispered. "It must have been left over from when Blow Frost's goons took over Brain Freezers. Victor obviously didn't notice it when he loaded the cart for us this morning."

"Is Hoff okay?" Lily said. "He looks kind of—freaky."

Hoff had finished eating now and was staring into space, a strange zombie look on his face.

Jackson shrugged. "He may have accidentally just eaten some of Blow Frost's mind-altering ice cream."

Lily's eyes widened. "Should we call his parents?"

"Nah," Quigley said. "It'll wear off soon. If we tell him to go straight home, he should be okay."

Jackson nodded. Then a slow smile spread across his face. "Wait—first I want to fix something. Hey, Hoff? Hoff Rockface!" he said loudly.

Hoff turned to look at him, his eyes still wide and staring.

"Hoff Rockface," Jackson said. "Wipe all photos of Jackson and Quigley off your camera."

Instantly, Hoff began doing as he was told.

"Wow!" Lily breathed. "That ice cream really works."

"Hoff Rockface!" Jackson said again. "When you've finished wiping the photos, go and wait in the park for Lily and the hatchlings. When they get there, give the little ones a push on the swings." Jackson gave a flippers-up to Lily. "Then—umm—go home. Oh, and try to be nicer to Jackson and Quigley, okay?"

"I'm not sure that bit will work once the ice cream wears off," Quigley said.

Jackson peered into the cart. "I wonder if there's any more in here? I could use some on Finola!"

"And your mom!" Quigley laughed. "Maybe

if we gave her some we could get her to agree to let us join the FBI."

"Ha!" Jackson sighed. "No amount of mind-altering ice cream would work on Mom. She's made of steel." He bent down to put his backpack under the cart. That's when he heard it—a loud crackle from the FBI radio inside, then a voice:

Jackson gasped. "Did you hear that?"

"Sure did!" Quigley said.

Lily frowned. "You guys aren't thinking of responding to that message, are you? Jackson! Your mom will go nuts! And what about the ice cream cart?" She looked at Quigley, then back at Jackson. They were both looking at her now, with hopeful faces. "What? No way!" she said. "Uh-uh! I am not working the ice cream cart for you."

"Please, Lily. Just for five minutes." Jackson made a pleading face. "City Museum is just across the park."

"Yeah," Quigley added. "By the time you've finished eating your ice cream, we'll be back."

"And don't forget Hoff's here to help you with the hatchlings," Jackson said. "Just keep telling him what to do." Jackson had slipped out of his ice cream cone costume and laid it on the cart. "I'll buy you another ice cream when we get back. Please?"

Lily rolled her eyes. "Okay, okay . . . I guess it would be fun to sell ice cream. I'm not wearing the costume, though; agreed?"

But Jackson and Quigley were already racing across the park, heading for the museum.

"Wonder what's happening over there?" Quigley puffed. "There's loads of valuable artifacts inside. Do you think someone's stealing them?"

"I dunno, Agent Q," Jackson said. "But something exciting is happening; I can feel it in my feathers. This could be our big chance to make the FBI see why they need us." He gave his buddy a flippers-up. "And this time Mom's not here, so she can't stop us. Come on! LET'S DO THIS!"